AFFAIR FOR
ETERNITY

BOOK 4: THE FINALE

C. Wilson

For autographed copies place orders on:
www.authorcwilson.com

LETTER TO MY READERS

Finally, I feel like I can breathe. This one here, like the others took a lot out of me emotionally. We have been riding this Bleek and Eternity rollercoaster for so long and now we have reached the end. So, thank you for rocking with me this far. Whew, Eternity and Bleek man. Y'all should know what I am about to say...

Get those snacks, drink, or smoke whatever your preference is. Put those little ones to bed if you have any and if you got a bae let em know that C. Wilson needs your attention for a bit. Buckle those belts y'all we are going for one final ride. This is the finale...

-xoxo-

C. Wilson

A Love Affair for Eternity Book 4 Playlist

What About Me, Lil Wayne ft. Post Malone

Used To, J.I the Prince of N.Y

Ice Cold, K Camp

Rise Up, Andra Day

I'm Not the Only One, Sam Smith ft. A$AP Rocky

Make It Better, Anderson .Paak ft. Smokey Robinson

Cry for You, Jodeci

Seasons of Us, Jagged Edge

Butterflies Pt. 2, Queen Naija

One Call Away, Charlie Puth

Imported, Jessie Reyez ft. 6LACK

Trenches, Monica ft. Lil Baby

Falling, Trevor Daniel

(I Hope You) Miss Me, Joseph Black

Let Em' Know, Bryson Tiller

Why I Love You, MAJOR

Promises, Phora

SAD!, XXXTENTACION

Fall Slowly, Joyner Lucas ft. Ashanti

Click here to listen→

*C*hapter 1

Bleek walked through the airport towards the arrivals exit. He wished he had taken his jet instead of flying commercial, but the trip was an in and out thing. He needed information and he damned sure got more than enough with his week stay in the Dominican Republic. The fresh air from outside danced across his face. His eyes had to register to the brightness of Miami. He squinted his eyes to block out the sun. As soon as he got his sights under control, he saw Paris running in his direction.

He put a smirk on his face as he dropped his bag and then opened his arms for her. They embraced and he welcomed the kiss that she had given him. Momentarily their tongues danced with each other. Her sweet peach scent invaded their space. After their kiss, he tapped her lips and then pecked her nose before picking his bag up from the ground and then walking towards the driver's side of the car.

"Babe I got it. I know that flight must have taken a toll on you."

Bleek was appreciative of Paris wanting to drive. He walked towards the rear of the car.

"Pop the trunk," he told her.

Once the trunk lifted slightly, he opened it and then placed his bag inside of it. After closing the trunk, he walked to the passenger side of the door and then got inside. Bleek turned around in his seat to face Tori. She smiled at him. He held a glow over his chocolate skin that only the hot Dominican Republic sun could give.

"Were my two favorite ladies playing well in the sandbox?" he made eye contact with Tori when he asked his question.

"Yes, we sure was babe," Paris said proudly.

Tori silently mocked Paris and then stuck her tongue out which caused him to erupt into laughter. *Be nice,* he mouthed to Tori. She rolled her eyes, so he playfully swatted at her knee before turning around in his seat. Bleek put his hand on top of the middle console and when Paris took her hand and intertwined her fingers within Bleek's he lifted their hands and then kissed the back to her hand.

"How was your trip?" Paris asked as she maneuvered her way through traffic.

"It was productive."

And that it was. He kept it short because still, Paris did not know that side of him. She knew Malik but she had no idea of his other lifestyle. His alter ego, that hood Brooklyn nigga named Bleek that was now a drug king pin. For months he had been trying to track down who was responsible for robbing one of his trucks. He knew that if anyone could have some form of information for him that it would be Julian, Tony, and Ty. He put his head back onto the headrest as he thought of his trip back to the Dominican Republic.

The hot sun beamed down onto Bleek's face. He took a seat on one of the lawn chairs in Ty's backyard. With an open beer in his hand the cold brew was the only thing that kept him from sweating profusely.

"The sun should be setting soon thank God."
Ty said as he entered his space. He sat in the seat that stood across from his brother.

"Nigga where the fuck ya shirt at?" Bleek asked once his eyes landed on Ty.

"It's too hot for all that shit."

"Well you need to do something ya old ass getting fat."

"Man," Ty grabbed his slight stomach that folded over the rim of the shorts he wore, "this is baby fat."

"I'm the only one allowed to say that shit."
Toya entered the backyard with a slight wobble.

"Come mere baby mama."

Bleek watched as Ty beamed with pride. He looked at his wife like she was the only woman in the world and to him, she was. Her round belly led the way over to him and then she sat into his lap.

"I can't believe y'all having another one."

"You need to catch up," Toya said with a smile.
Bleek breathed deeply. The loss of his son was not something that he had shared with his only family. He known that if he did, she would have never made the statement that she just did.

"Na, y'all have all the kids for me." He said as he pushed his emotions to the back of his lids.

"It's a boy this time. Finally, a boy so he'll be the third. We can nickname him Tre."

Ty had always wanted a son, but God had given him two daughters first. It was a clear sign that he needed to slow down and that he did.

"The third my ass I hate your name. We are not naming our son Tyshawn."

"Yeah aight. I don't give a fuck if I gotta dickmatize you into naming him after me, it's gonna happen."

Toya rolled her eyes as she let Ty talk. She knew that in the end she would fold to his request but that didn't mean that she couldn't put up a front, especially in front of Bleek.

When Julian entered the backyard with Tony and Kelsey at his side Toya smiled.

"Hi ma!" she greeted her mother.

"Hi baby!"

Kelsey and Tony had just come back from Aspen, so she had missed her daughter. Since their wedding, Tony and Kelsey had been traveling the world. Where others that were their age was sitting at home relaxing from years of working and just enjoying retirement, the newlywed couple was starting to live their lives by traveling the world.

"Y'all take that reunion shit in the house we got business to discuss out here."

Ty fussed as he rubbed his stubble beard. Toya turned around and then stuck her middle finger up at him.

When the ladies left the yard Julian and Tony sat in the other two seats near Ty and Bleek. Before sitting, they greeted the men with friendly hugs. It had been a while since they were all around each other. Bleek wished that his visit could have been more pleasure than business, but he had to get to the bottom of whoever was responsible for raiding his truck. It had always been a priority for him to find out who this person was but once they broke into his condo and then vandalized it, he was in a dire need to know who this person was.

"Okay now that they are gone, we can chat. We have never heard of a Chiva Blanca." Julian spoke for both him and Tony.
Bleek flared his nostrils.
"So, my trip here was for nothing?"
"Let me finish speaking son. We have heard of an Emmanuel Blanco though. He's from our era." He pointed to Tony and himself. Julian rubbed his hand through his slicked back silver hair before he continued. "He runs a Mexican cartel. If my memory serves me right… he runs his drugs right out of Tijuana and straight into California. I haven't even heard of Emmanuel in years."

"It's been about fifteen years or so," Tony added.

"Well what the fuck is his deal? I've been running my operation up and down 95 for the longest. What the fuck does some old ass Mexican nigga want with my shit?"

"Well, it could be Emmanuel and then again it could be someone else. Emmanuel was always direct so using the name Chiva Blanca isn't his style." Julian said and then sat back into his seat.

"You pissed off any Spanish mamas lately?" Ty asked jokingly.

"Ha ha hell, this shit ain't funny I lost a lot of money with that truck raid," Bleek said to Ty before turning his attention to Julian and Tony. "Is that literally all the info you have?"

Bleek's frustrations was evident. Some information was better than none but still it wasn't enough for him.

"Listen I have been turning over every rock trying to find out more but that's all I could come across. Malik understand that just how you took a loss with money so did I."

Bleek listened to Tony because he was right. Now that Julian and Ty was retired out of the game this problem on the table was Tony's and Bleek's.

"This is more than enough information bro, just know it's either this nigga or someone in his camp. You got to treat em how we would anyone else."

Bleek shook his head up and down to agree with Ty.

"Actually, you can't treat them how you would anyone else. Their operation is similar to ours," Tony spoke up.

"Well if that's the case how did y'all coexist back in the day?" Bleek asked.

Julian cleared his throat before he spoke up.

"Well, me and Emmanuel always had an understanding. He had the west coast while I took on the east."

"An understanding?" Ty interrupted, "Papa if y'all are on speaking terms squash this shit."

"Yeah, you talking about an understanding shittttt get him to understand that I'm not too cool on losing money. He robbed the wrong truck."

"It's not that simple. Me and Emmanuel fell out years ago."

"Years done passed papa I'm sure y'all can hash shit out to handle this situation." Ty said.

"I doubt it my boy, we fell out over Ma."

Ty and Bleek raised their eyebrows at Julian's statement. He was referring to his wife and they both knew it.

Tony on the other hand sat in his seat composed. He already knew the history between Julian and Emmanuel because he was there.

"Hold on... over ma? Explain."

Julian leaned back into his seat and sighed.

"Alessandra was Manny's girl, that's all I'm saying."

"Ooooo y'all was moving spicy back then?" Bleek finally spoke.

Everybody looked his way and chuckled until Bleek got serious.

"Julian please, you can sit down and talk with him. You and tia have been together forever, he gotta be over that shit. I'll even come with you."

Julian bit his bottom lip and then breathed out.

"Y'all are aging me. I'll set up a meet in Miami. I'll keep you posted."

"There we go now we solving shit," Bleek said with a smile...

Stopped at a light Paris looked at Bleek deeply.

"Did you hear me?" She asked.

"Na, ma what you said?"

"I said I'm glad your trip was productive."

"Yeah…"

Bleek turned the radio back up and then sat back into the seat. He pulled down the mirror and saw that Tori was sitting behind him engaged in her phone. After checking his face and then closing the mirror he sighed when he noticed that they had started to pull into traffic.

Chapter 2

Bleek entered his home with both Paris and Tori following behind him.

"What the fuck is all this purple shit?" he asked when he noticed the purple throw pillows that now covered the couch in his home.

"I did a little decorating."
Bleek turned around and looked at Paris with a sour facial expression. Tori chuckled under her breath and then made her way up the stairs and to her room.

"Purple ma? Really?"

"Well…" she ran her hand over one of the fur pillows, "you already have everything all white in here it just goes."

"Paris… I'm a fucking man. Why the fuck are there purple pillows on my couch?"

"They are lavender."

"I don't give a fuck if they were violet, get these shits off my chair. I already let you go crazy with the décor in the bedroom only because that's where you spend most of your time when you're here. Throwing ya feminine touch in *my* space is a *no* for me."

Paris' orbs started to fill with tears as she walked around the chair snatching the purple pillow from it.

"Well you have me staying here all of the time I wanted it to be comfortable for me. You're quick to act like this is my home too but when I start to treat it as such it's a problem!"

Tears cascaded down her pudgy cheeks as she grabbed the last pillow. Bleek breathed deeply before letting silence linger between them.

"First of all, stop yelling and secondly why the fuck are you crying?"

"I don't even know!" she quickly snapped as she wiped her face with the back of her hand.

Bleek figured that it was a territorial thing. Tori had just recently moved in and to him, Paris wanted to let it be known who the Queen of the castle was. He got it. He just didn't like how she went about doing it. He took a seat onto the white couch and then pulled her down on top of him. Which caused her to drop all of the pillows to the floor.

"My main problem with you decorating without me knowing is how these shits look," he kicked one of the furry boxed shaped pillows on the floor with his sneaker, "these shits are ugly."

"Shut uppppp," she giggled out as she continued to wipe her face.

He took his strong hand and then wiped her face clean. After all of the tears were gone, he kissed her forehead and then looked her in the eyes.

"I want you to decorate. I want you to feel comfortable here but just have a unisex state of mind when you do so."

"Okay..."

He puckered his lips and without a second thought she smashed her lips into his. After their kiss they remained nose to nose.

"You missed me?"

The way he asked in his husky tone wet her panties instantly. It was the deepness of his voice. It was the bulge beneath her that she felt and it was the racing of his heart beat that did it all for her.

"Yes..."

She did. The week-long vacation that he went on re-accompanied her with the vibrator that was her best friend before meeting him.

"Wanna show me how much you missed me."
She gasped when she felt his manhood jump beneath her. She loved when he did that shit, like a kid watching a party entertainer do their famous trick.

She didn't say a word as she stood from his lap and then grabbed his hand for him to follow.

"Mmmm, you on your silent sexy shit. I like…"
Bleek followed her up the stairs and then into his bedroom. When she pushed him into the room and then closed the room's double doors behind her he knew what kind of night was ahead of him. He smirked as she started to come out of her clothes.

***

When the sounds of moans could be heard through her closed door, Tori took that as a cue to make her exit. She quickly went to the bathroom that was attached to her room to shower. She had laid out a crop top and a pair of sweatpants to wear.

After getting out of the shower she tossed her natural hair into a messy bun and then started to get dressed. Her cell phone made a noise, so she picked it up from her dresser to check her notifications.

Jackson: what are you doing?
: I just got out of the shower. I'm getting dressed now

She knew that he would be calling her any minute. She had met Jackson in a supermarket a week ago and he had great conversation. She would occasionally tap on the line of flirting with him and she liked his style. He was store manager at a Publix and the total opposite of what Tori would have normally gone for. Considering the history she had with her *type*, this time around she decided to stray away from it. She was telling herself that a man like Jackson was probably the kind of man that she should have been settling down with this whole time.

Since coming to Florida, she realized that it was just like New York in sense. She ran into a couple of people she knew from back home which included one of her exes. A quick stroll down memory lane landed her with a sexual distraction, he was a bad boy with a rude mouth and when she saw him in a new city, she just had to see what he was about.

After the uncomfortable car ride from the airport with Bleek and Paris she was supposed to meet up with her ex-boyfriend before he left town to go back home but she changed her mind when Jackson texted her asking her out on a date reminding her of the goal she had set for herself. She wanted to leave toxic men alone and her ex-boyfriend was full of toxicity.

Jackson

After pulling her sweatpants over her derrière she looked down at the face of her phone to see who was calling.

"Hello?" she answered.

"Are you ready my love?"

He was too sweet with affection and she hated it, but she tolerated it because she knew that he had to be coming from a sincere place.

"Yup, I'm about to walk out now."

"You sure you don't want to text me your address and I come pick you up?"

"No, I'm fine I'll meet you at the movies."

Besides not wanting him to know where she lived, considering his occupation and his lifestyle the last thing that she wanted was for him to see how she was living. He lived a mediocre life and after all of the drama of her past she didn't mind it she just knew that all men couldn't handle a woman that had her own bag. To most, it was intimidating.

After grabbing her purse and her car keys she left her room. As she walked down the stairs, she still heard moans coming from Bleek's bedroom. *That's all they fucking do,* she thought as she made a mental note to start looking for houses. She was thankful for Bleek, not only had he took her in when she just basically jumped on a plane in one move, but he also filled her closet, helped with her business, and purchased her a car.

As she popped the locks to her Mercedes S-Class and then sat in the peanut butter colored seats she took a deep breath as she thought about her life and how the last year had been the most she had ever had to deal with. After glancing at her phone and seeing that she only had twenty minutes to get to the movie theatre before the movie started, she drove down the long driveway towards the gate to make her exit.

***

Tori found a park in the parking garage and then started to make her way into the mall. When she entered the movie theatre, she saw Jackson waiting at the entrance for her.

"Hey," he said with a warm smile.

His small round eyes became even smaller slits with the rise of his high cheek bones. He opened his arms for a hug, so Tori quickly gave him a half one and then pulled away.

"Come on."

He held his hand out for her and for a moment she just looked at it.

This was her first date since her break-up with Man-Man and she thought that she was ready for dating until now. As she stood in the lobby of the movie theatre, she started to regret her decision.

"I umm... I forgot something in my car let me go ahead and get it. Go and get the tickets, I'll be right back." Without even waiting for a response, Tori turned around and headed back out of the theatre. She pulled her phone out of her purse as she walked, she needed to speak to her sister. She knew that it was probably just first date jitters getting to her but, she couldn't shake the butterfly feeling in her stomach.

When it came to sex, she didn't second guess if it was too soon but to her having a date was the beginning of building something. For some strange reason, the encounter felt rushed. Or was it that she still had feelings for Man-Man, after all that they had been through she wouldn't be wrong if she did.

"Fuck," she cursed when she dropped her phone onto the tiled mall's floor.

When she picked her phone up from the floor, she saw that she had shattered the face of the phone.

"Fuck again," she mumbled to herself.
When she stood up straight and went to walk, she bumped into someone.

"Sorry," she mumbled before continuing to walk away.

When her arm was grabbed firmly, she turned around quickly.

"What the fu—"

"You should watch where you're going."
Sha stood in front of her with a serious look on his face. Her angry face lightened at the sight of him. His hair was grown a little and the shape up around his edges was sharp.

He was dressed in a calm fit, a white t shirt and a pair of designer jeans with a pair of designer sneakers to match.

"I said sorry," she said once she broke herself from the daze she was in while looking at him.

"No really, watch where you are going. You in Miami now, all that head in the phone shit need to stop."
Tori screwed her face and then placed her hand on her hip.

"I don't need a damn lecture from you Sha. I'm grown."

"There you go. Did you get what you needed out of the car?"

Tori looked over Sha's shoulder and saw Jackson standing there with a smile on his charming face. He was pretty boy with pretty features. He lacked the rugged look that she was attracted to which was another turnoff for her.

"I umm no I didn't even get a chance to go to the car ye—"

Sha turned in Jackson's direction when he saw Tori stumbling over her words. It was obvious that she was uncomfortable in the man's presence.

"Whatever y'all was about to do, ain't about to happen so beat it."

Jackson looked at Sha and then looked at Tori.

"Who is this?" he asked Tori.

"Really? This is what you about to do?" she asked Sha as she folded her arms across her chest.

"Hell yeah, this is what I'm about to do. You left me inside with our four kids to come outside and be with a bozo?"

"Four kids!?" Jackson questioned.

"Hell yeah, four kids and the last one is only two months old shitttt she ain't even done healing up," Sha quickly pulled his phone out of his pocket, "I can show you this video when she gave birth. That big ass head split her the fuck up."

Jackson's caramel colored face started to turn red.

"I did not sign up for this."

He turned around and then started walking back towards the movie theatre. When he was out of ear shot Tori finally started to let out the laugh that she had been holding in.

"Four kids! Really?" she held her stomach as she laughed.

"Shit, I had to say something you looked like you was running away from the nigga. He look like a lame anyway."

After getting her laugh out and then controlling her breathing she spoke.

"Thank you for that."

"Yea Ms. I'm Grown," he teased, "you're welcome." He went to walk away but the sudden interest in knowing why he was even at the mall to begin with piqued Tori's interest. When he had accompanied her on her shopping spree, he seemed to hate every moment of it, and she remembered him saying that shopping wasn't his thing.

"Hey," she called out which caused him to turn around and give her his attention.

"What are you doing in the mall anyway, you said you hate shopping."

"I do but my little sister's birthday is tomorrow. So, I need to get her a gift."

"You have a sister?" she asked, making conversation.

"Um yeah, I do have a family you know," he lightly joked.

"I could ummm help you pick something out."

She didn't want to go back home and being around
Sha felt comfortable, it felt like she was around family. He
didn't give her that weird butterfly feeling that she would
normally get when she was around strangers or around new
men. He looked at her for a while and that, made her
nervous. As quickly as she threw her invitation out there, she
wanted to snatch it back.

He stood in front of her with a blank expression as he
thought about the consequences of accepting her offer. It
could be two acquaintances just going shopping together. but
he would be a lair if he told himself that he wasn't feeling her
vibe. It was something about her. Those damn Washington
sisters had a vibe that was unmatched it was something about
their aura that drew the men around them in. He felt it, still
the curiosity in him wanted to be near her.

He knew that she came with a lot of baggage, besides
Bleek confiding in him her reasoning for even coming to
Florida the pain that she constantly went through on a daily
was evident. It spewed from her pores causing you to feel the
energy around her.

It was in her eyes. Besides that, when he had first met her in Chattanooga, she was toting around a round belly in front of her. He wondered what happened with that. All Bleek told him was that her old man had cheated and that she was starting over. The explanation for her living in the state now was clean cut with no real indication of what really happened.

He wanted to learn more, but he knew that with prying came the risk of her opening up to him. Was he really ready for that kind of commitment? A friendship where you knew the deepest, darkest parts of each other.

"Uhhh yeah, come on."

He had to take that chance. A slight smile spread across her face as he welcomed her invitation.

Chapter 3

"How does it feel baby sis?"

Tori stood in the middle of the open space with keys jingling in the palm of her hand.

"It feels damn good," she admitted.

She had so much left to get done but she was officially a business owner. The paperwork had been transferred from Eternity's name over to hers. She was scared but ready for the new challenge that would be ahead of her. The sound of her phone caused her to pull it out of her back pocket.

Big Sis: I just landed. I'm on my way to the hotel.

"What you smiling at?"

Bleek asked when he saw a grin appear on Tori's face.

"Nothing nosey."

"Yeah, aight. Don't let one of these Floridian niggas get killed."

That big brotherly protector instinct was peaking, and she knew that he meant exactly what he had said so she sighed after his statement.

"The people coming today to do the floors?" he asked changing the subject.

"No, I pushed that to next week because I want to paint this weekend."

"Did you set up the appointment with the painters?"

"Nope, I want to do it myself."

Bleek raised his eyebrow. The thought of Tori doing something like painting a whole hair salon on her own made him chuckle on the inside, but he held in his doubt.

"Well, why didn't you say something. I would have rescheduled my date weekend with Paris."

"I want to paint this weekend because I know you will be busy." Tori said with a smirk.

"Yeah, aight. You probably got a little nigga with his nose wide open to help you. I'm telling you right now, you better let him know who your brother is."

Bleek watched a sly smirk appear on Tori's face so he changed the subject. He knew that she was grown but he wouldn't be himself if he didn't elute his protective ways.

"Well, what do you need me to do today?"

30

"Just take the dresser stations, chairs and mirrors off of the truck out front. Oh, and the lights that go above the stations are in the truck too."

Bleek sucked his teeth.

"Why the fuck didn't you pay the extra to have the workers do this shit."

"Because I want to look around when this is done and say that family helped me piece it together."

"Shit... family helped you get the spot. Why the hell I have to slave after that?"

Bleek breathed deeply and then pulled his cellphone out of the back pocket of his jeans.

"Yo bro, get to Tori's shop in Miami Beach. She trynna slave a nigga."

Tori screwed her face. She watched as Bleek chuckled into the phone and then end the line.

"Who you invited over here?" she asked.

"Sha. Is that a problem?"

"Nope, no problem at all."

"I woulda wore some damn sweatpants if I knew that I was coming over here to work."

"You always wear sweatpants. That's like your signature outfit. You'll be aight wearing jeans and doing work. It's only for one day."

Bleek shook his head from side to side and then went to make his exit to start working.

Tori took the moment to go in the back where her office was located. The hot pink walls went beautifully with the glass desk that stood in the middle of the room. Alone she sat there for a moment just taking it all in. The thought of her upcoming grand opening brought her anxieties. Her worst fear was failing.

The sound of someone knocking on the open door behind her caused her to turn around.

"Bleek said do you want us to install the lights that go above the booths?"

Sha stood leaned up against the doorway. He came dressed to work. In just a white t shirt, basketball shorts and tennis shoes, he looked ready to move shit around.

"Get out ya head. You want us to install those ugly ass lights or no?"

Rude ass, she thought to herself.

"Yeah, y'all can do that. I'll be out in a minute."

He walked away without saying a word. Tori sighed to herself because things between them were so weird. She didn't know what to call it, but she knew that it excited her. The line of flirting and temptation was so thrilling. One day they would text all day while the next there was little to no conversation. She understood that cycle. He was a hood nigga and sometimes that's what came with it. She pushed her uneasy thoughts about the status of her and Sha to the back of her mind. She picked up her purse from her desk and her car keys she had to get up with her sister.

***

Tori stood on the outside of the hotel door with her duffle bag in hand. She had stopped home quickly to pack herself a bag.

"Tori Tee!" Eternity squealed as soon as she opened the door.

The two women embraced before Tori walked into the hotel suite.

"Well this room is lavish as hell, you got a balcony and all," Tori said as she observed the room.

"I mean it does call for a celebration. My baby sister is about to open her own business."

"About that…"

Tori smiled wide which made Eternity sigh.

"What you want man? You only put that smile on when you want something."

That look was the same look that Tori had been giving Eternity all of their lives. That one look would make Eternity say yes to anything. The big sister in her couldn't say no to that look and Tori knew it.

"Tomorrow can we paint the beauty bar together?" Eternity sighed and then slightly frowned her face.

"Tori, I already told you that I will be here for your grand opening next month. Now I have to be there tomorrow too? I really don't want to risk bumping into Malik at least not until the grand opening."

"You won't. I made sure that he would be busy tomorrow. Please sis…"

Tori added an extra sadness in her eyes as she slightly poked her bottom lip out.

"Alright fine. Ya ass is buying me some clothes that I can throw on and get dirty. I want to wear a denim jump suit like how them people that paint on the tv shows do."
Tori rolled her eyes as she laughed at her sister.

"We can do that. I would say that I can give you one of mine but we're not even the same size anymore. When the hell did you get all of this weight, huh?"

"Oh, this right here?"

Eternity turned around and then did a little twerk in her sundress.

"This that happy weight," she bragged.

"Ohhhh and she twerks now? Prince must be beating that up. Okayyy."

Tori raised her hand for a high five, but Eternity left her hanging.

"Actually, we haven't done anything yet."

Tori's mouth literally fell open.

"Ohhh, you out ya mind. It didn't cross your mind or anything?"

"It did but I feel like what we are building is beyond that. I haven't felt mind stimulation in a while and that's what he does."

Tori listened deeply. This new version of her sister was breathtaking.

"Hmm, well okay. Thought you was into the spirit of *to get over one you gotta get under the other.*"

Eternity screwed her face.

"Now, when did I ever give that impression?"

"It's how you move sis."

"How I move? Let's talk about how you move. You let weak ass Ty break your heart after I already told you what it was with him. After that you done ran down to Tennessee and fell right into the arms of Man-Man, we're not gonna get into that but what we will get into is now, somebody in that phone got you smiling and I bet it's a nigga. Thank you very much..."

Eternity said as she snatched the cell phone out of Tori's hand and then ran around the room.

"Give me back my phone!"

"Nope."

Eternity jumped on one of the beds in the room and then jumped off as she gave Tori chase and looked in her phone at the same time.

"Who is *Shooter Sha* and why are you sending him sexy pics?"

"Give me my phone!!"

Tori tackled Eternity onto the other bed. Eternity exploded into laughter as she watched Tori try to pry the cell phone from her grasp. Eternity let go of the phone to hold her stomach from laughter.

"Girlll..." she dragged.

"What knuckle head you met out here got you calling him *Shooter Sha?* Bleek is going to kill this nigga."

"Shutttt upppp!"

"Bleek gone kill him. Ohhh I needed this laugh."
Tears were forming at the corners of Eternity eyes as she
laughed.

"No, he won't cause he isn't gonna kill his best
friend."

"What?" Eternity's laughter came to a sudden stop,
"this Sha is not the same Sha that came to Chattanooga!"

"It is." Tori confirmed.

"Tori... how the fuck did this happen?"

Tori sat onto the other bed and prepared herself to tell
her sister how it all had started.

"We really just started vibing one day. I ended up
bumping into him at the mall one day and ever since then it's
like we're just in our own little bubble when we are
together."
Eternity listened intently. It was the look in Tori's eyes when
she talked about whatever it was that her and Sha shared. She
was scared for her sister because the pain that she had
experienced before she never wanted to happen to her again.

"Okay I'm here for it just as long as he doesn't hurt
you."

"I'm not even putting myself all the way out there for
all of that."

Eternity looked at her sister with uncertainty. She knew how quickly Tori could get wrapped up in her feelings. She hoped that she was serious with not putting herself all the way out there.

*CC*hapter 4

"Sis you fucking up when you paint. You have to do it on an angle. All the videos I've been watching that's how they do it."

Eternity rolled her eyes as she put down her paint roller and then walked over to the two flutes of champagne. She drank from her cup and then used a plastic fork to pick up a sliced strawberry from the nearby plate. She consumed the strawberry from the fork and then dropped two other pieces into her glass.

"Don't tell me nothing about some video you saw cause I could have hired professionals for you—"

"I come bringing tarps for the floor."

Both Eternity and Tori turned towards the salon door.

"Oh, thank you…"

Tori said with a weak smile as she quickly tried to meet the woman at the door. Eternity watched as the full figured, dark skin beauty stepped down the two steps in the entry. Despite the heels that graced her feet, the rest of attire was casual. She wore ripped jeans that cuffed at the ankle, a white wife beater and a long jean overall shirt covered her shoulders.

"What's still not done?"

His voice made a lump form in Eternity's throat.

"Hi, I'm Paris."

Eternity blinked away tears and then focused her attention on the woman that stood in front of her with her arm extended into a greeting. Eternity extended hers and their hands met into a formal handshake.

"I'm Eternity—"

"Paris go out to the car for me."

"Are we not helping Tori—"

"Go wait in the car for me."

Paris blew out a sharp breath and then let go of Eternity's hand as she turned to walk away. Eternity let the lone tear glide down her cheek as soon as Paris was out of the door.

"What are you doing here?" Bleek asked Eternity.

"What are you doing here?" she quickly countered as she wiped the falling tear from her face.

"I came to help her."

He pointed Tori's way.

"I came here to help her too."

Bleek closed in the space between he and Eternity. Tori stood on the sidelines and watched the two interact. It was heart wrenching. They did not know how to be regular around each other and it showed. She could feel the love and also the pain between the two. The moment looked as if it should have been a private one, yet her eyes were privy to see it. She could have gone into her back office to give them their space but watching was too damn entertaining.

So, she tucked the tarps that Paris had given her under her arm and drank from her champagne glass as she watched.

"Running into me wasn't a thought?"
He needed to know. Had he known that Eternity was going to be in town this weekend he would have sent Paris to her place. He damn sure would not have planned a weekend of dates and brought her to the shop had he known.

He was always in the dark, it was always a *had he known* kind of situation.

"She's pretty," Eternity said.

Bleek looked deep into her round eyes to try and detect sarcasm but he could not find any. Those eyes genuinely meant it. Paris' deep chocolate skin paired with his. Eternity wondered how deep they were into their relationship or whatever it was that they were doing.

She figured that it had to be pretty serious because he was bringing her around Tori. Eternity knew that this woman had to be the same woman that had been around her sister for months.

"You're beautiful."

He meant every word. The light sweat that glistened her forehead was covered with a streak of white paint. She had tainted her skin when she used the back of her hand to wipe the sweat earlier in the day. She blushed. His compliments would always put her in that state.

Nervously, she chewed on that bottom lip and badly he wanted to take it between his lips, but he wasn't a cheater and he knew that he would never be. Somehow, he knew that for Eternity it was possible. He knew that only for her he would skate shamelessly on the line of cheating but this time around before pursuing anything with her he had to know where her head was.

More importantly, he had to know where her hearts was. He had successfully restored his. Although he should have done it himself, but with the help of Paris, he was able to feel again.

"How long are you in town?"

He pushed the lose hair out of her face. She took note of the artwork on his outer hand and her knees became weak. This thug of a man tatted his skin for his loved ones. He would literally bleed for his loved ones so when they were gone, he bled for his loved ones in the only way he could, in the form of art.

"Only for the weekend."

"Let's do breakfast in the morning. Just me and you."

"Ummmm, okay."

"I'll text you."

He walked away from her and out of the shop, he had to. If he didn't then he knew that he would fall into that category of men that all women deemed as dogs. The category of men that he hated. There was too much fun in being single and doing what you want. He never saw the need to cheat. To be honest, he didn't hold down enough solid relationships to be even given the chance.

He needed the night to gather his thoughts. After sharing dinner with Paris, he cut the rest of their date night short. On the ride to her place, Eternity filled his thoughts. The slight weight she had now suited her. Her cheeks were fuller, eyes warmer, she looked happy.

"Where is your head? You wasn't into conversation at dinner and why are we at my house?"

"I need the night and possibly tomorrow."

"For what, may I ask?"

Her curiosity was peaked. This was supposed to be the day where they would wine and dine. The day that she looked forward to where they would just cut off the outside world. They both had terribly busy schedules, so she loved their date nights.

"Just give me tonight and tomorrow and then I will explain everything."

"Mmm," Paris groaned more so to herself, but it came out in an uncertain rumble.

He grabbed her chin and then turned her to face him before she was able to get out of the car.

"You're worrying the creases on your forehead. Chill out."

He kissed her pouty lips to calm her. She breathed out deeply after their kiss.

"Take all the time you need. I'll be here."

It was this kind of understanding that made it hard for him. She was so understanding to the point of him hating it. Eternity would have never, and this is why he knew that she was the one for him. Paris was a good woman, but she was a push over. Although she basically had it all, she was willing to eat shit from a man just to be happy and he couldn't get with that.

In a sense, in her past, Eternity had done the same thing when it came to Vincent but to Bleek she was a victim in that situation so he couldn't fault her for it. Any other woman in their right mind would have seen the tension in the room between Bleek and Eternity and would have questioned it. Paris on the other hand didn't, not publicly anyway.

She got out of the car, grabbed her Birkin bag from the floor of the vehicle and then walked towards her home. The two-story starter's home was more space than she had needed but it was a graduation gift from her father that she couldn't just say no to. Bleek watched as she swayed effortlessly towards her front door. He didn't pull off until he saw that she had made it inside safely.

He drove around Miami to clear his head. His travels ended him at the parking lot of the beach. He glared out at the body of water and sand that rested in front of him. He banged on the steering wheel in frustration. He sat there for a while. Images of Eternity plagued his mental. He tried to shift through his metal rolodex to find the good memories. Weighed against the bad, it didn't match up. He picked his cell phone up from the cup holder and then hovered over her name.

With the new cell phone number, he still requested that T-Mobile have all of his contacts transferred over. Deleting her number wasn't something that could be easily done. Although he knew that it would take nothing for him to get it back, Tori was always team Eternity and Bleek. He felt like it wasn't a coincidence that he had ran into Eternity at Tori's shop. Bleek knew that just like her sister, Tori knew him inside and out. There was no way that he would let her paint her store without him helping.

He blew out a sharp breath. Damn, seeing her had the same effect it always did on him. *Why?* He wondered why she pulled all of these emotions out of him. *How?* He wondered how she had been able to do it for all of these years. He had repaired himself. He had put together the broken pieces but looking at her, getting an up close and personal glance at her beauty, at her healing had him wondering how she had done it. He wondered if she accomplished that peace by her lonesome or if like him, she had someone helping her through.

Suddenly, he wished that he had pulled himself from his pain by himself. He looked at her name in his phone. It shouldn't have even been there, but it was. He always extended his hand for her. Badly, he wanted to call but he couldn't take the feeling that would come if she didn't answer.

: Wya?
A simple text. Three letters caused his stomach to hallow when he saw the three bubbles popping up with what could be her response.

She sent her location. She dropped a pin that he would surely follow. She didn't even have to text him anything, her sending her location meant that she was making herself accessible. Making herself available to him. He wondered briefly how she could have known that it was him, after-all he was reaching out from a new number. But he knew that the Florida area code that he was given was his tell.

He knew that they had a lot to talk about. He would be a damn fool to just think that they could continue where they had last left off without a talk. With his window rolled down, he heard the sounds of the ocean and it should have relaxed him, but it didn't. In the distance he heard the sounds of people partying. This is why he liked Miami because it was so similar to New York, so similar to the city that never sleeps. It was that familiarity that caused him to settle in this city to begin with. His heart was beating out of his chest as he clicked the location that was sent to him and then routed the maps on his phone to it.

A fifteen-minute drive. In that time, he could have changed his mind and gone home, he should have changed his mind and gone home but he didn't. He couldn't, he had to see her face. He needed time alone with just them two. He needed to feel her out. At first glance, he saw that something was different with her. It was her aura, or maybe it was the short cut that she was now rocking. It could have been the extra pounds that she had put on too. As he drove to the location, he thought of it all.

"Arrived."

Siri broke him from his thoughts. He picked up his phone from the cup holder and then sent her a text.

: I'm downstairs

Those three dots stalled his heart once more.

Eternity: Come up, I'm in room 718

Bleek read her text and then smirked. *Room 718.* She was so Brooklyn. Without even trying at that. Chattanooga and Georgia couldn't knock the roots from her.

He parked his car with the valet and then walked straight towards the elevators located in the back. He rode the elevators to her floor. With each passing ding, the spit in his mouth thickened. When the bell indicated that he was on the floor, he stepped out of the elevator and then searched for room 718. He stood in front of the door for a while before deciding to knock. With a balled fist he knocked twice and then stepped back to give himself some room.

When the door opened, Eternity quickly stepped out of the room and then closed the door behind her. He looked into her glossy round eyes and knew that she had to have been drinking.

"Hi," she whispered out.

Silence.

He didn't know what to say as he observed her. She was dressed more comfortably in a maxi dress that hugged her curves. She placed her hands into the pockets of the fabric nervously. He on the other side of the wall held his back against it to hold him up.

Being around her made him so weak and he hated it. He looked deep into her orbs and saw how the light coat of tears started to cover them. She chewed on her bottom juicy lip and he knew that the nerves in her caused her to do that. He knew so much about this woman that it was sickening to him. It never mattered how much time they spent apart he always would know all of these things of her. The makings of her was imprinted in his memory and he would probably never forget it.

"Are you going to say something?" she asked.

She was growing impatient with the silence between them and he knew it because her hand was placed onto her hip. She had that impatient motherly vibe going on, although she was in the wrong.

"How have you been?" he finally mustered up the voice to ask.

She expected to get cursed out but there he was concerned with her well-being. He would always be concerned with that shit when he should have been putting himself first. A damn fool in love.

"I've been... I've been surviving."

He knew that financially she was straight, she always had that go getter mentality. What he was speaking on was her mental health and that is exactly what he was asking about. Bleek wiped his hand over his fresh cut waves. When he did, Eternity saw the tattoo that was on his hand. She had noticed it earlier that day inside of Tori's shop, but this time around she wanted to show off her work as well.

She twisted her arm outward to show him her ink. She needed him to see that she had done the same. He smirked at her small dainty tattoo. Before that one, she had none. He knew every square inch of her body, so he knew that she was ink free prior to the tribute to their son. Where he was tagged up like the side of Brooklyn bodega, she was a clear canvas.

"I want to do more in his name," she admitted.
He had the same thoughts he just didn't know what to open. When he opened businesses, he sat down for months and thought strategically on what would be best to maximize his profits. But with this, with opening something for his late son, he didn't care about the amount of money that he would be pulling in. Opening that business was strictly to honor the name of his boy.

"I want to go back home and open up something like a YMCA, something that can help young boys. Something that can help pre-teens and teenagers period. I want a place that will minimize the amount of teens that get locked up back home. A place where kids can go to get away from a disturbed home life, somewhere safe."

Eternity's voice soothed him as she spoke. She was so excited as she spoke about the business that she wanted to embark on. He knew that this meant the world to her because growing up, she had experienced an unsafe living environment.

"We can do that."

Bleek loved the idea and couldn't think of any other place like home where they should start a business like that.

"So… your friend that came to the shop earlier?" she questioned as she tucked hair behind her pierced ear.

He wasn't shocked by her question because he was sure that Paris would come up as a topic of discussion for the night.

"Say the word."

He liked Paris he really did but Eternity to him was his one. Where Eternity was a diamond, Paris to him was a cubic zirconia. It was nothing wrong with her. She held confidence, she had her own everything and she had given him no other reason to believe that she wasn't loyal. She just wasn't Eternity.

"You would just drop whatever it is that you have with her like that?" she snapped her fingers.

"Absolutely."

Bleek wasn't for the games and he had never been. All of this she knew.

"So, what is it going to be?"

Before she could respond, the pocket of her dress rang. It was two in the morning so Bleek's interest was piqued with who was calling her. His face remained unfazed as he caught a glimpse at the face of her screen.

Prince

Beside the name was a football and a blue heart emoji. Quickly she shot the call to voicemail.

"Is that a friend of yours?" he asked.

Her eyes lifted from her phone screen and then met with him.

"Uhh, yeah."

54

She didn't know why she felt nervous answering the question. They were not together and hadn't been for a while and then to top it off, he had moved on romantically.

"What are we going to do about that?"

He spent too much of his prior years fighting for her love. He spent too much time fighting when she had always put him second when it came to other men. He would drop the world for her and in return she always questioned the thought of them, she always chose someone else over him. How was that fair to him? He was sick and tired of fighting a battle where in the end he ultimately always loss.

When other men were involved, he was always second, the safe choice, the choice that she would make after being dogged by the first. Those days were gone. If he was going to get her, he wanted her to turn herself over willingly. He wanted her to be so in love with him that she would naturally drop who or whatever just to be with him. Eternity tapped her cellphone within her palm.

She was madly in love with the man in front of her
and had been for years. She liked whatever her and Prince
had going on. It was pure and so untainted. Despite the love
she harbored for Bleek, she knew that with a past like theirs
he would always see her as flawed. He saw her at her
weakest moments, she had changed for the better but deep
down inside she felt like he still saw her for the woman that
she was, the flawed one.

With Prince, she could start fresh. She could do
everything the right way. The nagging feeling in her gut told
her that she should run away from him, that she should fear
what they could possibly be.

"Hey."

Eternity blinked her eyes when she felt her chin being
grabbed.

"You went in your head for a second."

"I'm sorry."

He looked deep into her eyes before invading her space. The
smell of his Tom Ford cologne attacked her nostrils and she
loved it.

"What are we going to do about that?" he asked
again.

His face was so close to hers that their lips touched with his question. She could smell the peppermint on his breath from the gum that he was chewing. That damn nagging feeling was screaming to her to walk away. What was done, was done but damn, she just couldn't move her feet. How could she walk away from who she loved most, from who she only currently loved? As his callused tips played in her scalp, she started to ignore that feeling.

That intuition was slipping from her. Quickly she was falling into temptation. Her history with Vincent quickly flashed through her mind. Although he was wrong in all that he had put her through, she was equally wrong for stringing him along knowing that her heart truly desired the man hovering over her. She didn't know what she and Prince had started but she enjoyed his company.

Without having any sexual ties or titles but she knew that if she were going to take Bleek up on his offer that she would have to let go of Prince all together. Badly, Bleek wanted to kiss her pouty lips. She stood in front of him in thought. He could tell that her mental knobs were turning just off the expression on her face. He looked her up and down and for a moment she thought that he heard the nagging feeling that was in her stomach.

Her ears heard what sounded like metal scratching together. She knew that it was all in her head but damn, why did her intuition had to feel like this? Why when it was the perfect time for them to be, did she have to start feeling like this? With his pointer finger he pushed some of her hair behind her ear. He sniffed in her vanilla scent.

"I can't repeat history. I need to let him go first."

"Okay…" he understood.

"I have to do the same."

For the first time he had someone besides her. He had someone that he had to let down easily. He hated that Paris had fallen in love with him but deep down inside he knew that this day would come. He backed away from Eternity, finally giving her the space that she owned. Na, fuck that, he backed away to give her the space that he owned. The space surrounding her belonged to him and had been since the day he had met her.

She felt like she could breathe a little easier. Being around him shouldn't have felt suffocating. You're supposed to be able to breathe easily around the one you love but after all these years, the butterflies in her stomach prevented that.

"Start looking for locations back home for our boy and then let me know prices. Handle that E and then hit me."

He entered her space again but only to lightly kiss her forehead. She watched as he swaggered down the hallway towards the elevators. That man had the illest hold on her.

In his younger years he was the wildest out there, yet she was able to tame him. Without even wanting to at the time, she was able to lock him down and have been able to ever since. As the elevator dinged, her stomach plummeted. She swore that every time he left her that there had to be a mass destruction somewhere in the world. She just knew that somewhere in the world thousands had to feel what she felt every time he walked away from her.

"Malik... wait."

He stood in between the doors of the elevator. The bells kept going off because he was standing in the way of them closing. After placing her phone back into her pocket, quickly she ran in his direction. When she collided her body into his open arms the new-found weight of her caused him to step back into the elevator. She smashed her lips against his as the elevator doors closed. He quickly pulled the button for the emergency stop as he kissed her back.

He pushed her body up against the wall of the elevator as he poured his love into her in the form of kisses.

"What... are... we... doing?" he asked in between kisses.

He was growing a hard one and he knew that once he took it out that there would be no turning back.

"I don't know. Just don't stop kissing me."

It had felt good, too good. It had been too long since she had been touched the way that he was touching her. In the confined space he was making her melt. He was making her loins feel warm. A slight moan escaped her lips which caused him to lick from her collar bone to the lobe of her ear.

"Stop with them moans. You trynna get fucked right here and now? You want all these lame bitches in this hotel on vacation for carnival to hear you calling my name?"

"Yes!" she admitted.

She missed everything about Malik Browne and that included the thick rod that he had in between his legs.

"That's what you want?" he asked again as he hiked up her maxi dress.

He gently rubbed his hands up her thighs in the process. She threw her head back in satisfaction ready to accept what was about to come.

Ding

Her phone dinging stopped him, quickly he went into the pocket of her dress to retrieve her phone.

Prince: just saw on the news that girls are getting snatched out in Miami beach, stay safe love.

He turned the phone for her to see.

"Handle that first before we do this," he handed her the phone and then backed away from her.

The text was innocent, but it showed compassion. Prince genuinely cared for Eternity and although it was flattering to her, Bleek wanted to kill him because of it.

"Stay safe love," he scoffed lowly.

She would forever be safe in the streets of Miami and that's because they belonged to him. He pushed in the emergency stop button and then the elevator started to descend.

"Malik, please just for tonight."

He had gotten her started and she yearned for him badly. He was tired of having pieces of her. He was tired of playing the back up to the back up.

"Na, not like this."

When the doors to the first level opened up, firemen were standing there looking at them.

"Are you okay?" one of them asked Eternity.

"Yeah, she good."

The man looked at Eternity with uncertain eyes. Her chest was heaving up and down and her maxi dress was hiked up over her thighs.

"Mam?" the fireman addressed Eternity again.

"Yes, I'm fine," she finally said.

Bleek shook his head and then sucked his teeth before pushing past the three firemen that was blocking his way. Eternity watched as Bleek made his way out of the hotel.

"Mam? Are you sure that he didn't hurt you?"

The distraught facial expression on Eternity's face made him ask her again, he had to be certain.

"He would never hurt me," she admitted as a lone tear cascaded down her face.

"Sorry about the alarm. Can I go back to my room now?" she asked.

"Uhh yeah."

The man backed out of the doorway of the elevator and then let it close in front of him

***

Eternity stepped off of the elevator on her floor and then leaned up against the wall as soon as she stepped out. She had to steady her breathing because the moment she shared with Bleek a little while ago was so intense. After taking a deep breath she made her way back to the room that she was sharing with Tori. She made sure to enter the room quietly because she knew that when she had left that Tori was sound asleep.

After a few drinks she would always knock out, that was the light weight in her. Gently, Eternity closed the door behind her.

"Where were you?"
Eternity almost jumped out of her skin at the sound of Tori's voice.

"I umm… I went to go get some ice."

"Oh, good because my head is banging. That damn alarm going off in the hall woke me up—" Tori paused when she didn't see an ice bucket in Eternity's hand, "well, where the hell is the ice?" she asked.

"I guess I forgot it."

"Who goes out for ice and then forgets it. And why are you sweating? What is going on?"

"Bleek came to see me."

Eternity said in a sigh as she plopped down onto her bed,

"Okay… and?" Tori asked as she leaned up and then placed her chin into the palm of her hand.
She was alert and she wanted all of the juicy details.

"We're going to open a business back home in Malik's name to honor him."

"Girl bye. That's business. A business discussion wouldn't have you hot and heavy like how you are right now. Go on, spill it…"

"Ugh," Eternity groaned, "We almost fucked inside of the elevator."

"Ohhhh that was y'all letting off that damn elevator alarm."

Eternity placed her open palm onto her face in embarrassment.

"Well… why didn't y'all?" Tori asked.

"Prince called me right before anything could happen."

"Mmm hmm and the plot thickens."
Eternity tossed a pillow Tori's way.

"Shut upppp," she whined.

"Listen, what are you going to do? It's obvious that Bleek wants to pick up where y'all left off. It seems like the ball is in your court."

Eternity knew exactly what she had to do. She didn't know how many more times that God would put her and Bleek together. She knew that she had to stop rejecting these times. Every single time she ran away from the man that she knew she was destined to be with she quickly regretted it in the end. She was tired of regretting things in her life.

"When I get back home, I'm going to let Prince down easy."
Tori looked at her sister and saw how she was in deep thought.

"You have a habit of going home to cut ties and you end up in a whole relationship."

Tori was into the fashion of keeping it real. She wouldn't have been herself if she didn't warn her big sister of the history she had been through.

"Well, for your information me and Prince aren't even in a relationship. We're just vibing."

"All the more reason to just ghost his ass. You want to give closure to someone that's not even yours. Like do you hear yourself right now?"

Tori had her own inner frustrations with the love story of Bleek and Eternity. If you asked her, they needed to be with one another and every single time they couldn't be she knew that it was all on her sister.

She knew that the couple had to be tired of the back and forth because she was tired of watching the shit. To her, it was the saddest soap opera she had even seen and growing up she used to enjoy watching General Hospital with Aunt Nora. Eternity swayed her head from side to side as she took in her sister's last statement. Tori was making a good point, but Eternity was tired of jumping from one relationship to the other.

If she were going to make things happen with Bleek this time around then she was going to make sure that they could co-exist first before they jumped into a relationship.

"His feelings are invested, it's the right thing to do," she finally responded.

"Well whatever then. I guess your mind is made up." Eternity chewed on her bottom lip as she watched Tori roll over in her bed to go back to sleep. Eternity was putting all of her eggs into one basket. She was betting it all on Bleek. It was time that she had. All of her prior choices had all been the wrong choices. This one had to be the right one.

: Handle what you have

She tapped her cell phone in the palm of her hand after sending the text. If she was going to end whatever she had with Prince she wanted Bleek to do the same. She watched as the three dots formed in their text messages.

Bleek: handle yours first

He was playing hard ball this time around. There was no way that he was dropping everything for her again. He had done it time and time again, so he was no longer willing to lose it all in return for someone who always chose the other option. He was no longer willing to start from the ground up emotionally how he always did when he dropped everything for her. She knew that this time around that she had to come correct because this time wouldn't be like all of the others.

Chapter 5

Tori's grand opening was just in two weeks. Eternity had ordered herself a nice dress to wear for it. The attire was a formal one and she was ready for the festivities. After setting some money aside in an account for Aunt Nora, Eternity was ready to leave Georgia and make her way to Miami to start all over again. Over the past couple of days, she had been looking for places out there. Not wanting to jump back into things with Bleek so quickly, she wanted her own place, that way Tori could move in with her too.

Tori had already promised her a job at the shop, so she was set with a steady income, although she didn't need one. Working gave her peace, it gave her distraction. She had only one more day left in Chattanooga before she was due to move to Florida officially. Bleek had already set her up with a plane ride on his private jet from Gwinnett airport to Florida. With just a room full of stuff she packed away her last box and then taped it shut. Bleek also made sure that workers would be able to pick up her things in a truck and drive it to Florida.

"You just about ready to leave this old lady already?"

Eternity turned around to find her aunt standing in the doorway of her room.

"Auntie Nora," Eternity sighed, "are you sure you don't want to come with me?"

She had asked her aunt before and she politely declined. Over the last couple of months, she had been the only person that helped her get through. Late at night when she stayed up crying from missing her son it was her aunt who cradled her until she fell asleep. On days where she didn't eat and would lock herself in her room it was her aunt that picked the lock to the room and basically spoon fed her to make sure that she ate.

"I'ma tell ya ass again like I told you before, I'm comfortable here in my little space. I ain't ready to learn another city."

Eternity rolled her eyes and then smirked. Her aunt, very much like her liked her privacy. Deep down inside she didn't know how she was going to adjust in Florida, but she was tired of fighting what she felt like should have been her life a long time ago. A life with Bleek.

"Okay fine… I'll stop bothering you about it. I just know that I am going to be worried about you when I leave. You'll be here by yourself again."

"And I was here by myself before you came. I will be okay. Listen…" Nora walked over to Eternity's bare bed and then took a seat, "I want to talk to you."

Eternity placed the roll of tape that she held in her hand onto the bare dresser that stood next to her. She turned around to face her aunt and placed up her back up against the dresser.

"What's up?"

She was trying to read her aunt. She had stress lines creasing in her forehead. There was an awkward silence between the two and a hallow feeling started to develop into Eternity's stomach as she waited for her aunt to speak.

"I wanted to let you know that your mother is really sick, and it would be nice if you and Tori try to visit her. She has been asking for you two."

Eternity screwed her face with attitude.

"Try and visit her? How do you even know that she is sick? I haven't heard from her in years. I was starting to believe that she was dead and now you're telling me that not only is she alive still but she's sick and requesting to see the daughters that she fucking gave to the wolves."

"Eternity baby, I know that you're holding onto some deep shit. I know you are baby, but you only get one mother. Over the years Machina has always made sure to reach out to me here and there, mainly for money but a few years ago me and her had a long conversation and something felt off about her. Her soul seemed troubled, you know? I felt it. It was more than just that monkey she always had on her back I knew that something else was wrong with her."

Eternity sighed as she listened to her aunt speak. No one knew exactly what she had to endure growing up. She held onto demons on top of fucking demons to spare her mother and to save her little sister. The last thing that she wanted to hear from her aunt was how after years of pain and abandonment that her mother, the one that was supposed to nurture and love her wanted to make amends.

"I don't give a fuck what's wrong with her. She doesn't deserve to be in the presence of me or my fucking sister."

"Now got dammit that's the last f bomb I'ma let ya little ass throw around me!" Nora lowered her tone when she saw Eternity shift her weight onto one leg. She cleared her throat and then continued, "the biggest pain that you can't rid of is regret. She's dying. All those years done caught up with that ass and the AIDS got her now. Every time we speak, she sounds so miserable. She sounds like all she wants to do before she dies is apologize to her girls."

"It's funny how life works like that. People are only sorry when it's a little too late. I'm good on visiting her. I will tell Tori and if she decides to go then that's on her but to me, my mother died the moment the judge sentenced me."

Nora looked at Eternity with sympathetic eyes. She still saw how her niece held onto the pain that her sister had put her through years ago.

"You are clinging onto this hate in your heart so stubbornly baby. It takes so much out of you to hate the next person. You need to let go and let God, Eternity."
Eternity rolled her eyes. She wasn't trying to hear what her aunt was saying. To her, only she understood the emotions she held towards her mother.

For years she cried in her cell because her mother didn't reach out to her. She cried because for years she endured the worst kind of pain and had she spoke up instead of trying to save her mother then maybe she would not have stabbed and killed a man trying to protect her sister. So many different scenarios played out in her head, all of them ending with at least her mother being there for her. She was hopeful when she knew she shouldn't have been.

"Did you hear me?"

When Eternity blinked her eyes, tears involuntarily fell down her cheeks. She focused her sights on her aunt.

"No, what did you say?" she asked.

"She's at Woodhull hospital if you change your mind or if Tori actually wants to say her goodbyes. I'll be up there sometime this month."

"Okay."

Nora stood from the bed and then walked over to Eternity. When she opened her arms, her niece hugged her tightly. Nora kissed the top of Eternity's head.

"I'm gonna miss you."

"Alrightt auntieee, you acting like I'm never coming back."

Eternity chuckled as she pulled away from her aunt's embrace. Nora gave her a soft smile because she knew that it would be a while before she saw her niece. This was the part in her life that she had told Eternity about over the past couple of months.

It was the part of the healing phase where she would be moving on. Where you healed is never where you stayed, and she made sure to tell Eternity that over and over again.

"Well look at the time, don't you have to go and tell that boy bye."

"Shitttt... I mean shoot."

Eternity had forgotten that she was supposed to meet Prince at his house in a bit. He knew that she was moving to Florida and requested that she come over for dinner before her flight in the morning.

"Gone head, fix yaself up to go break that boy heart. Don't make no damn sense."

"Auntie you said you didn't even like him. You said his beady eyes look sneaky."

"And they do... but still it don't mean he deserves to be kicked to the side for this other boy."

"He's not being kicked to the side for some other boy auntie. He's being kicked to the side for my own peace. I'm finally choosing what makes me happy."

74

"Ohhh yeah that damn rough neck that used to pick you up from the house when you was younger with the music blasting right?"

Eternity chuckled lightly. She was finally getting who she had wanted and the history between the two was insane. Ever since she had come home from serving her time, they had spent their days up under each other, that was until she started living the night life. After being locked away for so many years she had never wanted to be tied down, so she played Bleek at a distance.

"Yeah, that's him," she confirmed.

"Well he was a cute boy then, so I know time probably did him good."

"It sure did."

Eternity blushed as if he was in the room with her. Just the thought of him made her this way. It was a scary thing, but the feeling was so welcoming. Eternity's phone started to ring which caused her eyes to scan the room in search for it.

"Here."

Nora handed her the phone.

"Ohhhh this Prince guy even got the little heart emoji next to his name."

Eternity shook her head with a laugh before answering.

"Hello?"

"Hey hun, are you still coming by in a few?"

"I am," she confirmed.

"Okay… okay call me when you get outside of the gate."

"Okay."

She ended the line and then placed her phone onto the dresser in the room. She was expecting a chill night so besides the sweatsuit that she took out to wear for her flight the next morning she left out a pair of ripped shorts an over-sized t shirt and a pair of slides for the night.

"Alright let me get myself together."

"Mmhmm do that. You need me to curl ya hair for you?" Nora asked.

"Ummm no I think I'm gonna do a wash and go."

"A wash and go… as humid as it is outside by the time you make it down the stairs to your car you gone look like a damn troll doll. You better put a shower cap on and then just moose it when you get out the shower."

"Fine."

Eternity grabbed her underwear and then made her way out of her room to go to the bathroom. Nora followed behind her.

"Just think about what I said about ya momma too."

"Aight auntie, I hear you."

Nora rolled her eyes because she knew that her niece was not paying her any mind. When Eternity got into the bathroom, she turned on her shower water and then checked her text messages. She wrote back to Tori letting her know her flight schedule for the morning and to be at the private airport for her.

When she went to the message with her and Bleek she noticed that they didn't speak much. The last full conversation they had was two days prior when he had scheduled her flight for her.

So, she decided to call him. On the third ring he answered.

"What's up shawty."

"Hey..." she cooed.

He hadn't called her shawty in years. It took her back to back in the days. The young them, the them before all of the pain. The corners of her mouth curved upward at the pet name.

"What's up with you?"

She heard machinery being used in the background, so she knew that he was at one of his shops.

"Nothing I'm about to shower and go…"
She let her last word trail off because she didn't know exactly how to explain that she was going to break things off with someone who wasn't her boyfriend.

"Go where?"

"Go and speak to this guy. I'm just saying goodbye."

"Mmm…"

Bleek knew that this moment was going to come sooner or later. He kind of wished that she would have done it already, but he knew damn well that Eternity had a thing for doing everything last minute.

"Mmm?" she questioned.
She felt the tension on the phone as soon as she mentioned her going to say goodbye to Prince.

"You better not be going with a spendanight bag E, I'm dead ass."
Eternity started to laugh.

"You can't be serious."

When silence lingered on the line she spoke again.

"He and I never did anything there's no need for the tension you giving right now."

It was a soothing feeling to know that Eternity had not been sexual with the man that had been holding her attention but still to Bleek her going to say goodbye made him feel uneasy. He hadn't had *the talk* with Paris, but he knew what he wanted. Although he had been avoiding her since he had last dropped her home, which was the same night he had gone to see Eternity at the hotel during her visit.

When the line remained quiet, Eternity sucked her teeth. They were somewhat already getting off to a bad start. He lacked the faith that she had in cutting someone off. Rightfully so he had all reason to feel that way. She had a history of turning her goodbye moments *into I just need to make things work* moments and he was hoping that the night ahead wasn't one of those times.

"Well, I guess I will talk to you later since you're acting like you don't want to speak."

"It's not that I don't want to speak Eternity. I'm fucking scared. You have this thing with you where you want to spare any and everyone's fucking feelings but mine."

"Wow. You know what, you're right."

Eternity agreed with him. Over the years she had always cared about his feelings, but she knew that the way Bleek operated was off of actions only. Words didn't mean shit to him if the actions didn't match. Eternity turned off the shower water and then sat on top of the toilet seat.

"You're fucking right. I'm not going to say goodbye. It's not needed."

Bleek sighed into the phone.

"Na, I know you inside and out and certain shit you just have to do. I said this to you before with that other lame ass nigga I'ma say it again. I don't want you by default Eternity and I damn sure don't want you if the thought of someone else can ever linger in your head. I don't want you to finally be here with me but thinking about the what ifs with the next nigga. Handle ya shit man just while you handle it keep me in the front of that mind."

Eternity held the phone close to her ear as she listened. This is why she loved the shit out of the man on the other line. A piece of her still did not want to meet with Prince but she knew that if she didn't then he would wonder where her head was with him for the rest of their lives. She wanted to ensure him that this time around it was him and only him.

"Okay... what about you. What's going on with things over there?"

She didn't want to mention the woman that belonged to him, but she did wonder where he was with ending things with her. The slight moment of silence before he spoke was telling her that he was thinking of exactly what to say.

"I've been avoiding her. You know I don't lie to you and I won't start now I've been avoiding her until I know for sure that you are serious this time. I have uprooted shit for myself for you too many times and I'm not with that anymore."

"Okay."

It was all that she could say. How could she dispute or argue with facts? She knew that he was uneasy and she had all intentions of showing him that he had no reason to be. The woman that she was all of the years prior didn't have shit on the woman that she was now. She wanted pure love, natural shit and she knew that the kind of the love that she was seeking could only be given from Bleek.

"Mr. Browne, we need you in here a customer is complaining about the work done on his Lexus."
Eternity heard the commotion in the background.

"Tell the customer that I will be with them shortly..."

"Hello," he said into the phone.

"Go ahead, go and handle your business I will text you later."

"Okay, E."

"Malik... I love you."

"I know."

She had grown accustomed to his response. It was the guarded him. Over the years he had only told her that he had loved her when he felt secure in whatever they had. She had no doubts that he did, she just knew that he wouldn't say it openly until he felt that comfort within. She ended the line, turned the shower water back on and then got herself together for the night ahead of her.

Chapter 6

Eternity made a left onto an off road and then drove up a slight hill until her car was parked in front of a large black gate. From afar she could see the million-dollar mansion that rested on the land ahead. She had visited the house a couple of times within the last couple of months. Prince was a homebody and she loved that about him. He signed his contract, made his money, got injured while playing, worked hard as hell to make a comeback and did that. To her, his story was inspiring.

"Hey Siri, call Prince."

"Calling Prince blue heart emoji, football emoji…"

Before the phone could even ring the big black gates in front of her started to open. She knew that he must have been watching her on the cameras. She ended the call and then started to drive down the road that led to the house. She pulled behind one of Prince's cars, grabbed her purse from the passenger seat, grabbed her phone out of the cupholder and then got out of her car.

After placing her cellphone into her back pocket, nervously she used her hand to tuck her flat hair behind her ear. Like Nora had suggested, she slicked her hair down which gave her a flat look with curls at the end. Her face was bare and besides the clear lip gloss she wore on her lips. She walked up the three stairs that led to the front door and before she could ring the doorbell the front door swung open.

"Ohhh I'm sorry."

A woman with short curly hair that ended at her strong jawline said as she bumped into Eternity on the way out. The slight gray streaks in her head and the crowfeet at the corners of her eyes gave her age.

"Ma, I told you go out the back you don't listen." Eternity saw Prince walk up behind who she assumed was his mother.

"Eternity this is my mother, Perla."

"Hi Ms. Bontou."

She smiled at Eternity showing her pearly white teeth. She looked good to be his mother. Her body was snatched, and her face was youthful.

"You can call me Perla it's finally nice to meet you sorry I was supposed to be long gone but I ended up talking my son's head off."

Her smile was so warm that it caused Eternity to smile as well. She had no idea that she was ever a topic of discussion between Prince and his mother.

She watched as Perla leaned back and then kissed Prince on his cheek. After wiping the lipstick from his cheek, she walked around Eternity.

"Y'all enjoy the night."

She called out as she walked down the stairs and then got into the car that was in front of Eternity's.

"Can you get out?" Eternity asked.

"Yeah girl I know how to whip this shit."

Prince and Eternity laughed at her. Eternity now knew that his mother acted just as youthful as she looked.

"Come on."

Prince opened the door wider to allow Eternity a chance to walk past.

"It smells good in here."

Eternity placed her purse down on the table that stood in the foyer like she always did when visiting.

"I told you make sure you come hungry. On the menu tonight is soul food."

Eternity knew that in his home besides having a personal trainer on call that came with his home gym, he also had chefs on call that came with the huge kitchen that the mansion had.

"I will be damned if I eat some mac and cheese and collard greens from them white ass chefs that be cooking your food."

"Ha-ha, you got jokes, huh? I have staff here to serve us, but they aren't who cooked the meal."

"Then who cooked?" Eternity asked as she followed Prince through the house towards the dining room.

"My ma cooked."

"Ohhh check you out. You got momma love to come through and put it dow—"

Eternity stopped speaking when she noticed that the dining room was dimly lit with candles everywhere and rose petals on the floor. She felt a lump in her throat, so she gulped hard.

"I wanted dinner to be special since it's a special night."

Special night? What's so special about tonight? She thought to herself.

"Special? Uhh what makes tonight special?" She was stuttering over her words.

"It's your last night in town. You're about to go to Miami and embark on a business with your sister, that's admirable love."

He pulled out a chair at the table for her. She looked at him and saw that he was dressed comfortably in a pair of distressed jeans, loafers, and a button-down shirt. His locs was pulled out of his face and twisted towards the back of his head.

"Oh okay… well… we can't eat in the dark right?" On her way over to the chair she started to blow out the candles.

"Turn the light on," she added.

She didn't need the mood that he was trying to set for her. Like Bleek said, she was keeping him on the front of her mind.

"Um okay…"

After pushing her chair in after she sat, he blew out the last two candles and then went to a wall to flip the light switch on.

"Is that better?" he asked.

"Yeah, my momma always said eating in the dark is like eating with the devil."

She lightly chuckled because when Machina was in her prime, she was a good mother that yelled a long list of superstitious shit around the house.

Instantly she thought about the talk that she shared with her aunt earlier about her mother's health.

"Hey, you okay?"

Prince felt like she was off. She didn't greet him with a kiss when she entered his home which she normally would have done, and it was the aura about her. Something was troubling her, and he was curious as to what it was.

"Yeah, I'm fine."

"Okay," he didn't want to push her, "you ready to eat now?"

"Yes, I'm starving."

Her stomach had started growling as soon as she smelled the food upon entering the house.

Prince called out to the back and within minutes plates were starting to emerge from the kitchen. As soon as the plate sat in front of them Prince bowed his head and quickly prayed over his food. He always prayed over his food and he always did it silently to himself. He wasn't into the fashion of pushing his beliefs onto other people but he damn sure wasn't about to distance himself from his religion to comfort someone around him.

She smiled as she watched him. He was literally the definition of perfection. He loved his mother deeply, treated women with respect, prayed heavily and still had some hood in him. In a different life he would have been the perfect candidate for her but in this life, there was only one man for her. There was only one man that could make her swoon like how a woman was supposed to when she was deeply in love.

"Are you going to eat?"

Eternity looked up from the table and saw that he had already started to dig into his turkey wings. She smiled slightly and then pulled her plate closer to her.

Once she started to dig into her food her mouth watered for more. His mother could throw down in the kitchen. She had to have made the meal with love. After a half of hour of engaging in conversation and eating, they both cleaned their plates. Eternity unbutton the top button of her shorts because the pressure of the jean material against her full stomach was becoming too much to bare.

"Oh, you full full? There's dessert."

"I don't even think I can do des—"

"Amy!" he cut her off as he called out to the kitchen, "bring dessert please."

He loved to see her eat. In his life he was used to dating women that was scared to eat, they preferred salads with no meat in them. On their first date he took Eternity to a steak house and was surprised to see that not only did she kill her rack of ribs but the mash potatoes and broccoli with it was gone.

"Really Prince I can't even eat anymore and actually, I wanted to speak with you about something."

A white woman from the kitchen brought out a plate that had some kind of dessert on it with one candle sticking out of it. She smiled as she placed the plate down onto the table.

"Enjoy," she lightly said before walking away. Eternity looked down and saw that it was a slice of strawberry cheesecake, she had told him that it was her favorite. Around the rim of the plate in strawberry sauce written in script said: Will you be my girlfriend? When she looked up, she saw that Prince was smiling at her.

She now knew what the rose petals and his mom cooking dinner was all about. He was moving in the direction of wanting to commit and there she was only over to end whatever it is they shared. *Keep me in the front of your mind.* Bleek's voice played in her head.

"I umm… I have to go to the bathroom."

Quickly she pushed out her chair and then rushed to the nearby bathroom. After closing and locking the door behind her, she placed her hands on the corners of the sink and breathed deeply.

"Fuckkkk," she whispered to herself.

After turning on the water to the sink she pulled her phone out of her back pocket and then went to her call log. Quickly she tapped the name Malik and then held the phone to her ear. The phone rang three times and then went to voicemail. She hung up the phone and then went to their text messages.

: Tell me you love me... please

She watched as the three dots popped up on their text thread. When she saw that she called him again only for it to ring twice and then go to voicemail.

Malik: I'm handling what I need to like you are. I love you... you know this, come home to me Ma.

Once she read his text, she felt like she could breathe a little easier. He was doing exactly what she was, leaving who had her interest over these past few months. She felt better knowing that he was just as serious about them starting over as she was. She turned off the water, put her phone back into her pocket and then opened the bathroom door. She bumped right into Prince on the walk out.

"Are you okay?" he asked.

"Yes, I'm fine"

"What I did was too much?"

He needed to know. For the past couple of months, he enjoyed the hell out of Eternity.

She was smart, mature, beautiful, and caring. He had taken an interest in her so much that he had stopped dating other women all together. It was something about her that made him want to lock it down. He couldn't understand how a female like her could even be single, but he damn sure wanted to take her off the market.

"It wasn't. It was really sweet it's just that I'm not ready for that. I finally feel like I am about to live my life. I told you about my past. Going to Florida is going to be a fresh start after what was supposed to be my fresh start. I'm sorry, I hope you understand."

Prince remained silent for a moment after she spoke. He was taking in everything that she was saying.

"I get it. Listen, I don't want to lose you as a friend. You are really one of a kind."

He rubbed the side of her cheek and then stepped out of her way.

"Thank you for spending this night with me."

He was such a fucking gentleman dripped in ink, that followed behind the Lord's word, yet he was every little hood's girl dream. Not this Brooklyn girl though. She knew that one day he would make some woman incredibly happy, but it couldn't be her.

"Thank you for everything."

She meant it. Although he came towards the ending of her healing phase, he was a significant part of it. He showed her that there was other men out there besides Bleek that could be kind, gangsta and caring. She walked towards the foyer to retrieve her purse.

"Hey," he called out.

She turned around as she picked her bag up from the table.

"See you around Cinderella."

She smirked before walking out of the front door and out of his life.

Chapter 7

Bleek pulled into Paris' driveway and then cut his engine. He knew that she was home because her car was parked directly in front of his, besides that he could see that the light upstairs in her bedroom was on. He decided against calling her before he came over. He knew that she would want to talk over the phone and what he had to say needed to be said in person. He got out of the car and then used his key to lock the doors behind him. He took the house key she had given him off of his ring and then used it to enter her home.

He knew that it would be his last time using it so when he walked into the foyer, he placed it down on the accent table she had below the mirror that hung on the wall. Paris had taste, she knew how to decorate a home and she had a fashion sense when it came to dressing. He could hear the shower running from her bathroom upstairs. While tapping the post to the bottom of the stairs he was toying with the thought of leaving. He knew how quickly what he was about to do could get out of hand. Her feelings was invested and his was too. That is something that he couldn't deny.

He just knew that the feelings he had for Eternity could not be matched to whatever it was he felt for Paris. Knowing that, he took deep breath and then climbed the stairs. As he entered Paris' bedroom, he could hear her humming over the running shower.

"Ohhhh shitttt no no no no."

He raised his eyebrow when he heard what sound like panic in her voice.

"Yo P, I'm out here."

***

Fuck, Paris' eyes looked up from the pregnancy test she had in her hand. Lightly she walked over to the bathroom door and then locked it. Bleek had a thing for invading her privacy whenever she was inside of the bathroom. *Nice of him to fucking come around now,* she thought to herself.

"Okay, I'll be out in a bit."

She quickly tossed the positive pregnancy test back into the box and then threw the box into her bathroom garbage. After quickly washing she dried off, put on her terrycloth robe, and then opened the bathroom door.

Bleek sat on the bench that rested at the foot of her bed. She could hear him playing the Candy Crush game on his phone. She knew that something was plaguing his mind heavily. That was really the only time he opened the app and played. Little tell-tale signs she started to pick up on with him over the months and this was one of them.

"Took you long enough, I have to pee."
He stood from the bench, placed his phone into his pocket and then started to walk towards the bathroom that was behind her. She stepped out of his way. As soon as the bathroom door closed behind him, she cursed under her breath.

"Shit…"
Bleek walked over to the toilet and then lifted the lid. His nerves was a little bad and it was annoying the fuck out of him. In his mind he just knew that he could come over and break things off with her. He wasn't expecting to feel the guilt that was rumbling in his stomach. He aimed for the porcelain bowl and then relaxed when the sound of his urine started to fill it. As he looked down at the floor, he noticed the pregnancy test box in the garbage. By accident he turned his entire body while using the bathroom which caused him to piss on the floor.

"Fuck…" he mumbled.

He quickly aimed back towards the bowl to finish emptying his bladder. After shaking, he put his manhood back into his drawers and then he fixed his clothes. He cleaned up the mess he had made and then picked up the box out of the garbage. His hands was literally shaking. *There's no fucking way.* Silently he prayed. He dug into the box and pulled the used test out. When the plus sign looked back at him, he knees went weak. He put the test back into the box and then put the box back into the garbage.

Instantly his first thought was that she had to be messing with someone else because he had been careful their entire relationship. Then he remembered the nights where he was hurting. Those hard nights where she would be there to console him. Every single time he begged for her body to be near his, he entered her without protection. *Fuck...* When he noticed that he had been in the bathroom for too long he flushed the toilet and then washed his hands. Before exiting the bathroom, he needed a moment to himself. He always said that he didn't want any more children. The pain from losing Malik still weighed very heavily on his soul. He couldn't fathom going through that pain possibly twice.

He opened the bathroom door and saw that Paris was dressed in pair of cotton pajamas. She sat at the head of her bed Indian style.

"Did you take all the space you needed?" she asked.

"Actually no. I want to talk to you."

"Okay… let's talk."

She had felt the change in him, and she just knew that this was the talk that he was probably avoiding for the longest.

"Well for starters—"

The ring of his phone caused him to stop speaking.

"Sorry," he apologized to her because he rarely kept his phone on ring.

He saw that it was Eternity calling him, so he shot the call to voicemail and then placed it on silent. Shortly after, the phone vibrated in his hand. He went to his text messages and saw that she had sent him a text.

Eternity: Tell me you love me… please

He started to text her back but as soon as he started typing, she called him again. He shot this call to voicemail and then went back to the next message.

: I'm handling what I need to like you are. I love you… you know this, come home to me Ma.

There was no way that he was going to not let her come to Florida. He knew that he would figure everything else out later but what was priority on his list was getting her back to him.

"Ah hem," Paris cleared her throat, "are you done?" she asked.

Her attitude was evident.

"Sorry," he apologized again before locking his phone and then placing it into his pocket.

"You were saying?" she asked.

She wanted to get the inevitable over with. She knew that he was about to break up with her. She felt it. She had felt the disconnect for a while, but she ignored it.

Being with Bleek was so up and down. Some days he felt like he was all in while others he was so damn distant. He had been even more distant ever since they both had run into the woman by the name of Eternity inside of Tori's beauty bar. She didn't even know the woman, but she was familiar with the name. While helping Bleek heal it was the name he constantly called in his sleep. She remembered that a year prior when she had answered his phone that it was Eternity that had called. She blocked Eternity's number and thought that would be the end of her.

"I think we both know that this isn't going to go any further than what it has been."

He spoke with no emotion and that part bothered her. She wondered how it was so easy for him to throw away what they had. Instead of beating herself up about it she owned it. Coming into the relationship she always felt off, she knew that the feelings she desperately tried to pull out of him would probably never be reciprocated. That's why she overly compensated with her understanding with him. After months of trying to understand, she started to grow tired of how he handled her. He showed his interest when he wanted to, and she hated that shit.

"Okay… is that it?"

Bleek placed his hands into his pockets as he just looked at her. He couldn't read her. He expected her to throw shit, scream something. The calm shit scared him a little. The break-up was easier than he expected but still, he couldn't leave that house with knowing that there was a positive pregnancy test in the garbage in her bathroom. That would be him doing the same shit he did with Eternity, ignoring that nagging gut feeling.

"You pregnant?"

He tried to read her facial expression.

"I just took the test a little before you came."

"You weren't going to say anything to me?"

"What is there to say? I'm not keeping it."

"You not doing what?"

His voice was louder than what he intended it to be. He blew out a sharp breath before he continued.

"So, because I don't want to be with you, you're going to kill my seed?"

"Tuh."

She started to laugh which pissed Bleek off.

"I just started my career. A baby is the last thing on my mind especially from a nigga that is barely around."

There was the low jab. Now she was showing her hurt. Her emotions was starting to come out.

"Paris this isn't something that you decide on your own."

"I just did though..."

She was testing him and they both knew it.

"Now is that all that you came over here for?"

She was young and, in the moment, it was showing. It was obvious that she was only speaking on an abortion because he didn't want to be with her. If that is how she wanted to live her life, then it was fine with him.

The situation to him was literally one less headache. After poking his bottom lip out and then shaking his head up and down he pulled his lip in between his teeth and then started to head towards her room door to leave.

"And you're just going to leave?" she cried out. Quickly he turned around frustrated.

"What the fuck do you want from me Paris!?" She jumped at the base in his voice. His eyebrows scrunched in anger. She had no idea that the topic of children was a sensitive one for him because they had never discussed children before.

"I want to know why."

"Why what!?"

He couldn't calm down even if he wanted to. She had shown him a side of her that she never showed before. She was being petty with a life all because he didn't want a relationship with her. To him, it wasn't respected. A woman with motherly tendencies didn't do shit like that. He knew that if she were to keep the baby that she would be one of those bitter ass baby mamas and that is not how he saw his life with having children. So, if she wanted to visit Planned Parenthood then so be it to him.

"Why fucking take me on this emotional ass rollercoaster knowing damn well I was never it?"

Bleek looked around the room but remained quiet. He didn't have an answer for her. He didn't know why he strung her along this long. She scoffed.

"Nigga don't have an answer for that then answer this… is it because of Eternity?"

The normal poker face he wore on his face broke.

"What do you know about her?"

"Wow…"

Tears streamed down Paris' face.

"You just answered the question for me. I know that while I was stupidly helping you get through whatever the fuck it was that had you broken, at night you would call her name. I know that she had to be the same woman that was at Tori's beauty bar because you haven't been the same sense and I know for fact that she is someone from your past because last year she called your phone and I answered. I guess me blocking her did nothing…" she mumbled the last part to herself.

Still, he heard her loud and clear.

"You did what now?"

He walked closer to the bed because he could have sworn that he heard her wrong.

"I said what I said…"

"This is really who the fuck you are, huh?"

He chuckled, which threw her off guard.

"What's funny?" she asked.

"You... you're fucking funny. This person that you are it takes all of the energy from you. I know it does. It has to be exhausting to live life as a fucking fraud. I thank you though, you did help me heal. Helped me heal really good. Now I can be a better man for her, so thank you."

"Fuck you Malik!"

Paris picked up the clock that stood on her nightstand and threw it in his direction. He dodged the hit.

"There she goes... toxic ass bitch. I'll send you whatever money you need to handle that shit. Ain't no way you pushing out anything of mine. I'm not about to be in a toxic ass cycle with ya ass and let me say this, you not about to have any second thoughts about this shit either you said an abortion is what you wanted KEEP that same energy."

He turned around and then headed out of her room door. He could hear her crying, but he didn't give a fuck. In his mind he was trying to figure out when Eternity could have possibly called him the year before. He prayed that it wasn't before their son had gotten kidnapped by Vincent because if it was, then Paris blocking Eternity from calling his phone was kill worthy.

If she had blocked her calls before his son's death, then that meant that Eternity was possibly reaching out because she wanted to leave Chattanooga. If that was the case, in his eyes Paris had an unknowingly hand in his son's death. He walked out of her house and then quickly walked to his car.

Eternity

As soon as he got into his car his cellphone connected to the Bluetooth.

"What's up, ma?"

"I did it..." she sounded like she had lifted a weight off of her chest.

He chuckled at her excitement.

"I love you Eternity... come home to me."

"I fucking love you more Malik! I'm coming, baby. How did it go?"

Eternity knew that him leaving the woman he was with would be a little more difficult because they actually shared a relationship. She was a strong believer in you lost a man how you got him but, in her eyes, Malik was a loaner for the woman he was with. He belonged to her and they both knew it.

"It went ... well it's done."

That's all she needed to hear.

"Okay. Well that's all that matters. I'm back at auntie's. I'm gonna try and get a nap before this flight."

"Okay, ma. I'll be at the airport for you."

"Na it's okay Tori is going to pick me up."

Bleek drove effortlessly on the freeway as he spoke.

"Why can't I come get you?"

"She's really excited about me finally moving out there I just figured that I would let her be the one to pick me up."

"Well she gone have me riding passenger because I'm coming Eternity, she's not the only one that's excited."

"Okay."

Eternity couldn't stop smiling. She was finally doing this. Her and Bleek engaged in small chit chat as he drove home.

"I don't even see her car, hold on E let me text Tori really quick to see where she at."

"She's out with a friend, she's fine."

"A friend? It's fucking three in the morning."

That protective trait in him kicked in fast. Tori was indeed his little sister. Blood couldn't match to the bond they had.

"Babe... she's in good hands, trust me."

He sighed and then grabbed his phone and got out of his car.

"Aight man, I'm believing you."

Bleek put his phone on speaker as he undressed and placed it onto his bed. Eternity was talking his head off about this house she had found that really liked. In his mind, she was moving in with him and that wasn't up for debate, so he let her continue to talk about the marble countertops and the view of the water. When he heard the FaceTime noise on his phone he walked over to the bed. He smirked when he saw that it was Eternity FaceTime calling him. He pressed the green button and then walked to his bathroom.

After propping the phone up against his bathroom mirror, he grabbed his toothbrush and toothpaste.

"Hey beautiful."

She was smiling at him. She loved to see that tattooed frame. He was shirtless and only wore his Versace boxer briefs. As he brushed his teeth, she just observed all of him. She hadn't been touched in so long and in the moment, she missed him, she craved him. He grabbed his nearby rag and then washed his face. He smiled into the camera.

"My jibbs is good?" he asked as he smiled.

"Mm hmm"

She was laid in the bed with her hot pink bonnet on.

"I like ya little chef hat."

She started laughing loudly.

"Girl you better take ya ass to bed and get off the phone with that boy before ya miss ya godddamnnn flight! You kekeing like a goddamn Cheshire Cat. He not even that funny."

Eternity covered her mouth to stop her laugh from being heard. She didn't even know that her aunt was up.

Bleek chuckled.

"She's right ma, is your alarm on?" He asked.

"Yeah it is."

She turned over in bed and then placed the phone onto the pillow next to her. He got into his bed and did the same.

"Aight then go to bed."

"You first."

"Shitttt I'm up."

He fluffed a pillow under his head and then yawned.

"You're not," she said before she yawned.

In no time he was snoring into the phone and for a while she just watched him. She was grateful that they had come to this space. She knew that they had been working on themselves, but it was time to put in overtime to get them to work while being together. Just as good as it felt to be with him it could quickly turn bad if one of them turned to the blame game when it came to losing their son.

"I love you," she whispered before he hung up the phone.

She tossed and turned for a few hours before she finally drifted off to sleep.

***

The alarm going off caused her to jump out of her sleep.

"Ughhh," she groaned.

She reached over and grabbed her phone and saw that it was ten in the morning. She had seven missed calls from Bleek and three from Eternity.

"Fuckkkk."

Tori had missed picking Eternity up from the airport. She felt him staring at her.

"So, you couldn't wake me?" She asked.

"I wasn't about to wake shit. When that first alarm went off you was slapping the fuck out of that phone plus I spoke to Bleek and he said he got her, so I let you sleep. He also said that he was looking for your ass so that means you didn't have that talk with him yet, huh?"

"Ughhh," she sighed again as she pulled the covers off of her body.

"Sha, I've been over here since we started whatever this is, I haven't gotten around to it."

"Mmm, I told you before this even got here that he's my mans and that it should come from me, but you insisted on it coming from you. I'm not waiting on you anymore."

She rolled her eyes and then tried to get out of the bed, but he grabbed her by the waist and pulled her back ono the comfort of his king-sized bed.

"This shit is mine Tori and you gone stop walking round this bitch like it's not."
He grabbed her crotch and then bit his bottom lip as he hovered over her. With his thumb he messaged her clit through her lace panties.

"Sssss," she lightly moaned.

"Okay… come on I gotta get ready."

"Leave ya car here let me drop you home."

"No…" she moaned out.

He slid her panties to the side and then inserted two fingers into her garden while still massaging her clit with his thumb.

"I'm telling him today."

"Okayyy."

He had captured her mentally and sexually he learned her body so quickly and owned the shit. She still had a lot going on with her harbored emotions for Man-Man, but Sha understood that history didn't erase overnight.

He recognized the hurt in her and never tried to ignore it. He knew that for the moment she was in love with someone else. Even though she was wrapping herself in Sha they both knew that she still loved Man-Man deeply. He just offered his help. He was okay with being that body that got her over the last body because he knew that his vibe was intoxicating. She would fall for him sooner or later. She was just currently guarded.

"Okay?" He questioned.

He leaned down and kissed her neck while still playing with her pearl.

"Fuckkkk yesss."

He smirked. He knew how to work her body to get her to agree to anything. He took his fingers out of her garden and then sucked her juices from them.

"Aight let's go."

Tori shot her eyes open and then leaned up to push him down onto the bed.

"You really wanted to start with me, huh?"

She pulled his strength out of his boxers, slid her panties to the side and then eased down onto his shaft.

"Mmmm," he hummed.

"Why you like starting with me?" she asked.

"Shitttt."

He grabbed her hips and navigated her. He loved that she matched his sex drive. With both hands on the top of his headboard she used that as leverage to snake her body on his python.

"You gone stop using sex to get answers out of me. Ima tell him."

She wrapped one hand around his neck as she lifted and dropped her lower half onto his member. She was bitching him, and he was starting to feel like he had to nut. He grabbed her hips and then rammed his dick into her.

"Ahhhh fuckkkk."

"What the fuck did I say Tori?"

He used one hand and played with her tit through one of the t-shirts of his she wore. She threw her head neck in satisfaction.

"Okay…" she folded, "I'm cumming," she admitted.

"Me too…"

"Fuckkkk," he groaned as he filled her walls with his essence.

She laid into his chest and they both breathed deeply.

"Aht aht."

She was famous for going straight to sleep after she caught a nut.

"Get that ass up. We gotta go."

He wanted to get her home, have the heart to heart with Bleek and then start his day.

"Fineeee," she whined as she got off of him and then rushed to the bathroom.

She ran the shower water before sitting on the toilet. She was nervous about Sha telling Bleek about them, but she knew that it was time. She was starting to come home less and less, and she was running out of excuses to tell Bleek.

***

Eternity walked around the kitchen preparing breakfast. She felt uneasy and she couldn't understand why. She was finally there in his kitchen in just one of his shirts. She was home yet her soul didn't feel at peace. Once he picked her up from the airport earlier that morning she showered, got into more comfortable clothing, and tried to attempt to make herself at home.

"Are you ready to talk about what's bothering you?"

The sound of his voice soothed the worries in her mind. Finally, she had pin-pointed what was troubling her, it was her mother. When she felt the warmth of his body behind her she leaned back into his embrace. He rested his face into the crook of her neck and looked down at the stove at what she was cooking.

"You look good as fuck in this kitchen, E."

She knew that he loved to see her cook, especially wearing one of his shirts.

After taking the last piece of turkey bacon out of the pan, she turned around and offered him a weak smile. He put his hands onto the island counter and then lifted his body to have a seat.

"Come here."

She came, she always would. Standing in between his legs she let him embrace her.

"We not about to do this bottling up shit. If anything is worrying that head, I need you to get that shit out."

"It's my moms…"

Bleek wasn't expecting to hear that. He was sure that whatever was bothering Eternity had something to do with him. He knew that her mother was a sensitive topic. As long as he knew her, he knew that their relationship was nonexistent. Hell, when he had first ever laid eyes on her she was roaming around Brooklyn in hopes of finding her mother. A teenager fresh out of a detention center yearning for mommy's love.

"Okay what about her?"

He put his listening ears on. In conversations he always gave his undivided attention

"Before I left Chattanooga my aunt told me that she's sick and dying from AIDS. She asked if I could go see her, me and Tori."

Bleek knew that recommending that she say her goodbyes wasn't as simple as black and white. The history she shared with her mother was a difficult thing and he knew how stubborn Eternity could be.

"Well what do you want to do? We need to go back home to handle this youth center. We have to start looking at places. I'm not saying you should see her but if it crosses your mind while we're up there then why not? How long does she have?"

"I don't know. Two weeks or a month give or take."

He heard the sadness in her tone.

Losing a parent never felt good it didn't matter if that parent was good for you or not at the end of the day that was still your parent. He could relate to what she was feeling though. His own mother never fed his spirit but still, when she died, he felt the pain of the world on him. He harbored regret for hating her for so long.

"Well Tori's grand opening is in two weeks we can go to New York next week. I already have a realtor looking at commercial spaces."

"Okay…"

She still didn't even relay the message that Nora had given her to Tori. She didn't know how her little sister would feel about their mother dying. But she knew that she had to tell her. Out of the two, Tori was more emotionally attached to Machina.

"Hey hey, I'm walking in the house. Making my presence known just in case some freak shit is going on." Eternity and Bleek looked at each other and laughed when they heard Tori's voice.

"We're in the kitchen," Eternity yelled out.

Tori entered the doorway to the kitchen and then stopped when she saw that her sister was only wearing a T-shirt and panties.

116

"Sha is with me sis."

Eternity's eyes opened wide and then she went to make her exit through the other doorway in the kitchen but not before Bleek pulled her in and kissed her forehead. Once she was out of the room Tori entered the room with Sha trailing behind her. Bleek reached into the bowl that rested behind him and pulled a green apple from it.

"What y'all doing rolling in together and Tori where the hell were you?"

"Tori go catch up with your sister let me talk to my mans."

Nervously she looked back at Sha before looking at Bleek who was still waiting for an answer.

"I um… man I'll just let him talk to you I'm tired of this shit."

She walked away to go and find her sister.

"Aight… let's talk."

Bleek already knew where the conversation was heading. Eternity had told him Tori's whereabouts without even telling him. The night before when he worried about her, she told him to trust her and that she was safe.

Bleek knew that Eternity knew him inside and out. The definition of the word safe wasn't generic with him. For someone he loves to be safe that person had to be with someone he trusted. Being that Tori and Eternity were sisters with a bond stronger than gorilla glue he knew that Tori probably told her sister the tea of her and Sha first.

Sha was the furthest thing from intimidated, but he knew that the topic would be an uncomfortable one.

"Me and Tori is a thing."

"Aight."

Bleek shrugged his shoulders and then took a bite of his apple. Sha looked at Bleek deeply as he tried to read him. Not wanting his friend to be in thought for too long after taking another bite of his apple he finished speaking.

"You know the kind of shit she been through, just do better. That's it, that's all."

"No doubt, she not like these other bitches out here bro. She make a nigga feel like she the reason God still love me. That's the way I see it. She's a sign that God still fuck with a nigga, word."

Bleek started to laugh but he understood. He felt the same exact way about Eternity.

"How the fuck you show your thankfulness for God and curse in the same damn sentence."

"You know me bro, I keep shit real as fuck."

And he did. This is why Bleek had no ill feelings towards the pair being together.

"Oh listen, next week we need to take a trip to New York."

"New York for what?"

"Me and E about to open a business there and it's some shit with their moms. I need you to come because I don't know what kind of head space Tori gone be in if they decide to see their moms. She been through too much in the past year, Eternity too. Shit like this could fuck around and break them."

Sha shook his head up and down.

"Aight I'm down."

"Oh yeah, before we go though, I have a meeting with Julian and possibly whoever Chiva Blanca is."

"Aight I'm down for that too."

"Na bro, I don't need you present for that I'm just letting you know one of these days when I tell you I need you to step in at the shop in Fort Lauderdale that's the day of the meet."

"Man, you not about to be walking into no shit doley I'm coming."

Sha leaned up against the doorway to the kitchen.

"I won't be doley, Julian will be there with me and he ensured me that it'll be a clean meet."

Sha looked at him uneasily.

"Aight anymore fucking news?"

Bleek chuckled, "na, that's it."

Chapter 8

Bleek sat in his parked car outside of a Mexican bar and grill in Miami Beach. His gun rested on his lap. After sighing he pressed a button on his steering wheel that opened the air vents above his dash screen. It was a secret compartment for his weapon. After putting his gun into the slot, he pressed the button again to close it. Julian ensured him that the meeting would be a clean one, but something just wasn't sitting well with him.

A black Maybach with deep tints rode past him and then parked directly in front of the restaurant. He saw the chauffeur get out and then open the back door for someone. Julian exited the car and then fixed his suit jacket once he stood straight. Bleek watched for a moment before he got out of his car. He remembered admiring the man in front of him when he was a young boy.

Those were the times when it was just him and Ty nickel and dime bagging it in the streets of Brooklyn. To be where he was now was a blessing in rare form to him. Most hustlers was on the street forever. They weren't given the chance to be at boss status like how he was, pure king pin shit. Besides that, they either encountered jail or death and he had slid past both effortlessly.

Bleek got out of his car and then locked his doors. When he saw Julian step aside, he noticed that someone else was getting out of the car. As he walked over his face held confusion. He didn't bring Sha because he thought that it was just going to be him and Julian. When he noticed that the man that got out of the back of the car was Ty, he held a sense of relief. His uneasy state disappeared instantly.

"Fuck you doing here boy boy?" He asked once he was in ear's reach.

They dapped up before Bleek embraced Julian in a hug.

"I wasn't letting this old man come out here by himself and I wanna know what's up with this Mexican nigga. Tony was trynna come but I told him stay inside with the girls and shit," Ty explained, "you ready?"
Both Julian and Bleek looked at him.

It was Julian that was setting the meeting, but it was Bleek's job to headline the shit. He was in charge and no one could run his shit.

This is what he hated about being the one that everyone came to. This is why he hated being boss. He had to have the answers and with this situation ever since his 18-wheeler got robbed he hadn't had any. In situations like these he missed New York. Being in the streets was a jungle anywhere but at least back home in New York it was a jungle that he was used to. Still, he had to keep his shit together because this is what he had always wanted.

After putting in all the work in his younger years it was only right that he be placed in the position that he was now in.

"Yeah, let's do this."

"Stay parked here," Julian said to his driver before leading the way to the bar.

When the trio entered the establishment, it was empty. Only one Mexican man stood behind the bar wiping down the counter. It was late but still during hours of operation. They knew that Manny had to have closed down the business for this meeting.

"We closed," the man said without looking up.

Julian chuckled.

"Tell Emmanuel that there's a SUV no tints with two spare tires waiting for him."

The man let go of the rag he was using to wipe the bar down and then looked up at Julian. Without saying a word, he walked through the double doors that was behind him and into what looked to be the kitchen.

Three men came out of the double doors with assault rifles trained on Julian, Ty and Bleek.

"He said he only ordered one spare tire!" one of the men with a gun trained in their direction said.

"The fuck is this?" Bleek mumbled under his breath. Julian stood calm and relaxed with his hands in the pockets of his dress pants.

"Emmanuel has always been a pussy," he mumbled back.

"Gentlemen, where is Emanuel? I told him that I was coming here in peace."

Julian opened the jacket to his suit to show that he held no gun on him.

"This is not only a waste of my time, but it is also disrespectful," he added.

Ty and Bleek stood back and watched as Julian spoke. They had never saw him in this element and if this is how he was in the streets then they both understood why he ruled the game for so long.

"You come in peace, yet you bring an extra body with you..." one of the men said.

A short Mexican man with a floral print shirt on and a cigar hanging out of his mouth pushed through the three men that stood in the double doorway with the assault rifles.

"You still have this fucking mouth eh?" He asked Julian.

Julian smirked as the man walked his way.

"Was that supposed to change Emanuel?" He asked.

Both men smiled at each other before they embraced.

"Put those damn guns down," Manny said to the men behind him.

"You ain't got shit on you right?" Manny asked with a raised eyebrow.

His gaze shifted between Julian and the pair that stood behind him.

"I'm clean."

"But are they clean?" Manny asked.

He stared at Bleek for a while after his statement.

"They are," Julian confirmed.

"Aighttt meng… y'all going through that metal detector so for y'all sake I hope that's true."
Manny's heavy accent kicked in as he waved his hand for the men to follow him.

"Move out tha fucking way," he said to the group of men holding guns as he walked past the double doors.

Julian followed behind Manny while Ty and Bleek followed behind him. Once behind the doors and successfully though the metal detectors all four men sat at a long rectangular table in an empty warehouse space that rested in the sublevel of the establishment. Manny sat on one end while Julian, Ty and Bleek sat on the other end.

Manny traded in the cigar he had in his mouth earlier for a toothpick. He ran his hand over his slicked back jet black hair.

"Julian, I appreciate you coming with no tints but buddy… the extra spare tire I knew nothing of."

"Yes, and I was only coming with one, but my god son insisted on taking the trip with me," Julian said as he nodded his head in Ty's direction.

"Ahhhh Tyshawn senior's boy he was a good meng."

"Yeah he's loyal just like his old man but," Julian nodded his head towards Bleek, "this man right here is who needs the answers."

Manny chewed on the toothpick in his mouth as he listened.

"I just might have some answers. Julian you didn't say much over the phone. So, you meng... what's up?"

Bleek chuckled in his head at how Manny said the word *man*.

"Julian tells me that you used to go by Manny Blanco... there's a Chiva Blanca on my ass. One of my trucks got robbed and my condo got broken into and trashed. I know that you have been out of the game for a while and what I'm asking for is a long shot, but do you know who Chiva Blanca is?"

Manny sat back in his seat and rubbed his stubble beard. He reached into the pocket of his shirt and then pulled his phone out of it. Bleek cocked his head to the side, he was waiting on a response from Manny but the man across the table from him seemed to be too occupied in his phone.

"Ahem," Bleek cleared his throat to disturb the man that was scrolling around in his phone.

Manny put one finger up as to tell Bleek to hold on, pressed a button on his phone and then placed the phone onto the table. The phone ringing on speaker filled the silent room.

"Hey Tio, what's up?"

"Chiva... have you been busy my dear?"

Bleek's eyes lit up at the woman's name. He tried to pick up on her voice but to him she did not sound familiar.

"You sure you didn't piss off a Spanish mama?" Ty leaned over and whispered to Bleek.

"I'm fucking positive now shut the fuck up so I can hear," he whispered back.

"Well what have you heard Tio?"

"Chiva.... You are beating around the bush my love. You of all people know how much I hate that," Manny said as he rolled his eyes.

The line went silent. Knowing that his niece was stubborn, Manny knew that he would have to reveal his hand to even get her to talk.

"I have a young man sitting across from me right now saying that a Chiva Blanca robbed one of his trucks and trashed one of his homes. Is this true my dear?"
She chuckled into the phone which pissed Bleek off. Julian laid a light hand on his shoulder to silently tell him to relax.

"So, you must be sitting across from someone named Bleek, eh?"

"How the fuck you know me?" Bleek asked, unable to hold his composure.

"Tio, we will discuss this later. What I will say for the dirty bum to hear right now is that no one will keep me off his ass. This is about revenge and it is personal."

"Personal!? Bitch I don't even know you."

"Bro chill," Ty said to Bleek.

"Na fuck that!" He stood from his seat.

The woman on the phone laughed. It was a sinister chuckle that was pissing Bleek off even more.

"You took something from me Bleek. It is only right that I do the same you know. Tio I'll be in touch."

Before Bleek or Manny could say anything, the woman hung up the phone. Manny sighed and then shrugged his shoulders.

"Stubborn family meng... can't control them."

"Man, she's talking bullshit. You really about to let your niece rage a war over some nonsense?"

Manny sat back in his chair, clasped his hands together and then rested them on his round belly.

"The war is hers to fight not mine."

He was unbothered and it showed.

"Was there anything else you needed to know?" he asked.

Bleek sniffed his nose in frustration.

"Na, I'm good. We can fucking go," he directed his last statement towards Julian and Ty.

Both men stood from their seats, preparing themselves to follow Bleek out.

"Julian…" Manny called out, "don't let another twenty past before reaching out you hear? We should do this more often and next time bring Alessandra along with you." Julian looked at the smirk on Manny's face and then lightly chuckled.

"She'll be happy to be present. I'm sure she wouldn't mind putting the bullet in between your eyes that I couldn't twenty years ago. Stay healthy Manny."

Julian was the last to exit the room. He thought that the meeting would be more productive for Bleek but after hearing the hatred in the woman's voice over the phone he knew that there was nothing more that he could do for Bleek. It was up to him to get to the getting before he got, got.

Chapter 9

Bleek skillfully drove through the streets of Brooklyn as if he had not been gone for two years. Eternity sat passenger in his Benz. Still after all of these years he kept his apartment in the Bronx. It had been where they were staying since they had been back home. Tori and Sha had stayed in a hotel since the apartment was only a one bedroom. He glanced over at Eternity and saw that she was staring out of the window. He grabbed her hand and then gave it a gentle squeeze.

"You good?" he asked her.

He knew that her mother had to be on her mind. Especially since he had just driven past her old neighborhood.

"We should go and see her tomorrow, well you and Tori."

Eternity let out a dramatic sigh. She wished that he had not known her as well as he did. If he didn't, he would not have been able to take a hint at what was bothering her.

"I'll think about it. Today can we just look at this spot and pray for the best. The last three businesses we saw since we've been here just didn't feel right."

"Okay."

He wasn't going to push her, but he did know that before they left New York that he wanted her to get her closure with her mother. There was no getting closure once the person was dead and he understood that. He didn't want her walking around with that burden weighing on her. In his eyes she already had to walk through life carrying so much, she didn't need anything else added.

Bleek brought the car to a stop, put it in reverse and then parked in the empty spot outside of the center. On the corner of Bedford and Monroe in Bedford Stuyvesant there was a YMCA that had been closed for almost a year. No one had purchased the commercial space and to Eternity it was the perfect spot. It was next door to a high school and in the heart of the area. The couple got out of the car and then walked to the building.

"Hi, Mr. and Mrs. Browne?" a woman wearing a chocolate pant suit asked as soon as they entered the building.

Eternity turned around and looked at Bleek. The name that she was called was flattering and she knew that he had everything to do with it. He smirked and then shrugged his shoulders. To him, no one else was fit to be his wife so anyone that he did business with would not call her anything besides that.

"Yes, that's us," he said in his strong tone.

He then extended his hand for a shake.

After the woman firmly shook his hand, she left her hand out to shake hands with Eternity.

"Okay, so like I was telling you over the phone. This space has a pool, a gym, basketball court and it also has a garden sitting area located in the center of the building. There are four floors. Some upstairs have classroom settings and others are empty. Here on the first floor there is a full kitchen area. The Y used to serve lunches afterschool for Bedford Academy right next door."

She led the way around the establishment showing them every single room. Eternity's smile gave Bleek the confirmation that he needed. The location was perfect.

"We can sign paperwork…"

"We can?" the realtor asked Bleek with a confused look.

"Yes, we can." Eternity confirmed with a smile.

"Well okay, let me go out to my car and get the paperwork. I'll be right back."

The woman exited the room and when she did Eternity looked at Bleek with a smile so bright that it warmed him.

"Are we really doing this?" she asked.

"We are..." he confirmed.

She ran in his direction and then jumped when she got close to him. Without struggle, he held his arms open for her and let her jump onto him. Her thick legs wrapped around his center. He cupped under her ass as they kissed. This shit, this was the tempting shit she had been doing over the past week.

The kisses, the hugs and when they laid in bed, she would toot that rump on his dick and it would drive him crazy yet, he respected her body. She hadn't given him a sign of her wanting to be intimate yet, so he wasn't going to be with her.

"I'm back... oh sorry," the realtor apologized for interrupting.

"Na you good."

Bleek placed Eternity onto her feet.

She wiped the gloss from his lips that she had put there with their kiss. While Bleek and the realtor handled the paperwork, Eternity went outside to get some air. She had yet to tell Tori that their mother was sick. She reached into the purse that hung from her forearm and took her phone out. It rang in her ear twice before her sister answered.

"Hello?"

"ToriTee where you at?"

"I'm showing Sha around. We in Harlem now getting some seafood what's up? Did y'all find a spot?"

"Yeah we did. Remember the YMCA that was on Bedford and Monroe?"

"Oh, hell yeah! Remember we walked all the way from Boys and Girls to Bedford Academy when I was in school because them girls said they was gonna jump me?"

Eternity chuckled. She had remembered how when she had first come home from the juvenile detention center that her sister always kept her in the middle of some drama. When she had just come home Tori was a Junior in high school. She was a popular girl that had a lot of mouth. Knowing that her big sister was coming home, that mouth only intensified.

"Yep... I remember. We have the Y right next door to that school."

"That is a good look sis. I'm happy for y'all. We was gonna come over today anyway. I'm tired of eating out. Can you put Bleek's kitchen to use?"

"Yeah I can do that," Eternity knew that Tori loved her cooking, *"but listen this isn't why I called."*

"Okay so what's up?"

Tori tried to pick up on her sister's tone, but she couldn't.

"Tomorrow I need you to come to Kings County with me."

"Why what's wrong?"

Eternity picked up on the worry in Tori's tone.

"I'm fine but Machina isn't."

"What's wrong with mommy? Wait how do you even know something is wrong with her?"

Tori, although distant from her mother never detached the name from her.

"It's a long story. Auntie Nora has been keeping in contact with her over the years and she told me that she's sick. She's dying and Nora thinks that we should find some time to say our goodbyes."

Tori remained silent on the line. Eternity knew that a phone call wasn't the way to tell her this news, but she had to do it while she had the courage to. She didn't know how she would feel the next day or even within the next twenty minutes. So, telling Tori about it could at least put the burden she had been carrying since talking to Nora on someone else.

"So, what do you want to do?" Tori asked.

Now, Eternity was the silent one on the line.

"I mean like... I'm telling you so you can say your goodbyes."

"I'm not going without you."

There it was, the guilt trip sister shit that she really needed to make her go.

"Listen... y'all relationship and her and mine are different I wouldn't feel any way about you going to get closure ToriTee."

"I said what I said... I'm not going without you."

It was that stubborn shit right there that she had taught her baby sister.

"Ughh," Eternity groaned.

She lightly jumped when she felt someone wrap their arms around her waist but then relaxed when the gentle breeze blew the smell of his cologne towards her nostrils.

"We'll talk more when y'all get to the house tonight," Eternity said into the phone.

"Okay fine."

Eternity hung up her phone and then dropped it into her purse. Bleek kissed the nape of her neck and then held a set of keys in front of her face.

"You ready for this?" he asked.

"Yesss."

She snatched the keys out of his hand and then turned around to face him.

"Tori and Sha is coming to the house tonight. She wants me to cook. I told her about my mother too. So, we might be going to the hospital tomorrow."

Bleek looked at her and was shocked. He thought that he would have had to fight her to get her to go and see her own mother.

"You better make some good shit tonight too. I want baked mac and cheese."

"That's all you ever want when I cook."

She playfully rolled her eyes and then led the way to his parked car.

"That's cause you make that shit like how my grandmoms used to. Like what the fuck y'all be putting in that shit."

He opened the car door for her and then waited for her to get in. After closing the door behind her he circled the car and then got into the driver's seat. They had solidified step one to opening their new business which was the location. He had lawyers, interior decorators, and advisors for everything else. Knowing that classrooms was on the third floor of the establishment Bleek already had it made up in his mind that he wanted to hire teachers and mentors to help the kids with their homework if needed.

He even wanted to make sure that a psychiatrist was on payroll to be there. Growing up in Brooklyn as a young boy he had held so much of his shit in because before meeting Ty he had not had anyone to vent to. That by itself created a monster within him, it made him ruthless. If he could stop that cycle for other boys out there, he was all for it.

"What's on your mind?"

Eternity's voice broke him from his thoughts.

"You making a mess in my kitchen. I want you making messes in my kitchen for the rest of our lives."
She smiled because his statement was as romantic as he was going to get.

"First of all, I clean as I go."

"Please aight, the only thing you clean is a fucking plate because you the only person in the world I know that can eat and cook at the same damn time."

Eternity rolled her eyes and then laughed before playfully slapping him on the shoulder.

"Shut the fuck up and take me to a grocery store."

He smiled before turning the music in the car up. He figured that they could go to the supermarket down the block from his apartment.

***

"Tell me what I can do to help."

Bleek was pleading with Eternity. They stood outside of her mother's hospital room, but she just could not go in. Nora was inside and Tori was late as expected. After a night of soul food, drinks and playing cards, her and Sha had left Bleek's apartment during the wee hours of the morning. They had planned to visit the hospital at noon because that's when Nora told Eternity that she would be there.

Ever since waking up that morning Eternity felt like she should have backed out of trying to make amends. Even while walking to the car before coming she had chills, which could have been from the New York's fall weather, but she was as superstitious as they came so to her, it was a sign.

"I can't walk in there without my sister," she admitted.

Nora being there was one thing, but she felt like she needed the strength of her baby sister to get her through what she was about to do. Nora knew of the way Machina raised the girls, but Tori was in that house living it with her. Without saying a word Bleek reached into the pocket of his jeans, pulled his phone out and then placed a call to Tori's phone.

"I'm here I'm here don't be calling me."

Eternity lifted her head and smiled when she saw her baby sister approaching them. Bleek and Sha dapped up and quickly Bleek gave Tori a hug. Sha leaned up against the hospital's hallway wall like Bleek. Both men were there for support, so they played the back and just let the ladies take the lead.

Tori peeked into the window of the hospital room.

"How long has auntie been in there?" she asked Eternity.

"About an hour."

She looked at her sister and noticed that Eternity was rubbing her hands together nervously.

"Welp, her time is up. We need to get this shit over with."

Tori opened the door and when she did the room reeked of urine. She curled her upper lip over her nose.

"Auntie we know you probably staying until visiting hours are over, but we're not so do you mind if we have our moment really quick."

Nora looked Tori's way and then sighed when she saw her niece's facial expression. Upon walking in the room Tori had not given her mother any attention until she spoke.

"Tori..." Machina's voice was raspy it always had been.
She coughed a couple of times before calling her daughter again.

"Tori..."
Tori turned her head in the direction of her mother. She was the mirror image of Eternity just with a darker shade of skin.

Even with the drastic weight loss she could see that her mother still held her gorgeous features. She just knew that it was the reason why she was able to sell her body for drugs as long as she had been doing.

"What?"

"Tori—"

"Nope, Nora let her get her shit out..."
Tori crossed her arms over her breast as she watched her mother and her aunt speak.

Nora stood from her seat and then prepared to exit. She was expecting for Eternity to be the one to bring all of the thunder upon entering the room, but she saw that her youngest niece was the one bringing the storm first. When she walked out of the room her eyes landed right on Eternity. She could tell that she had been crying because her eyes were puffy. She knew that more than anyone that she had mixed emotions when it came to her sister.

She crossed the hospital's hallway and then wrapped her doting arms around her niece.

"Alright baby... okay..."

As she rubbed Eternity's back, she looked at both of the men that stood on each side of her.

"Which one of you are Bleek?"

The dark-skinned man to her right leaned up off the wall and gave her his attention.

"You got her?"

If only she knew just how bad he did have her.

"I got her," he assured.

"Aight now cause she been through enough and I don't mind the Florida scene. Fuck around and come kick ya ass if anything happens to my baby."

Sha chuckled under his breath which caused Nora to look his way.

"Oh, auntie don't play I'll kick ya ass too just cause you know him."

"Yes mam," Sha said with a smirk.

Nora broke the embrace from her niece and then cupped Eternity's face with her hands.

"Go in there and let go. All this heavy shit you feel on your chest gotta go."

Eternity shook her head up and down to agree with her aunt. Nora wiped the tears that was falling down her cheeks.

"You hear? Let it the fuck go."

Nora kissed Eternity's forehead and then swiped the lose hair out of her face.

"Better make sure she good."

Nora jumped at Bleek and then smiled softly before walking down the hallway.

"Your aunt acts just like you."

Bleek was amazed at how young Eternity's aunt looked. Eternity wiped her face clean and then smiled.

"Yeah, that's where I get all my spice from."

"Shitttt…. Well then where the fuck does Tori get hers from?" Sha asked as he shook his head from side to side just thinking about Tori's personality.

"She gets that shit from our moms…"

Her last word trailed off as she said it.

"You ready to go in there?" Bleek asked, changing the subject.

"Yeah... can you come in with me?"

"Of course, I can."

Without a second thought he agreed.

"Come on," he knew that she needed that little push.

He held his hand out for her and she took it. He led the way to the closed room door and then with his unoccupied hand he opened the door.

"Did your sister come wit—"

Machina's voice caught in her throat when she saw Eternity walk into the room with a man accompanying her.

"Eternity..."

Bleek stood back and watched the interaction. He could feel the tension in the room. A mother was supposed to take care and protect her kids but the woman lying in the hospital bed had not. The resentment in the room could be felt too.

"Machina..." Eternity answered.

"My girls."

Machina tried to sit up in the bed, but she was too weak to do so. Bleek walked over to help her sit. Eternity cut eyes at him. but she decided to stay silent. It was the good in him that went to her assist and that was a part of him that she had loved. Once Machina was in a comfortable position she spoke.

"I wanted to apologize to you both… I know that I had fucked up with raising you but I just couldn't die without telling you both that I love you…" she paused and then put the oxygen mask on because she was running out of breath while speaking, "I know you both hate me but I'm still your mother and I just thou—"

"You're still what?" Tori had heard enough.

When she was younger, she always had hope in their mother, and this is why the lack of parenting that Machina showed throughout their life always got to her the most. Eternity on the other hand had lost all sign of hope when it came to their mother.

The very first day where she was sold to the highest bidder, her hope in her mother went out the window.

"Let me tell you something Machina that *I'm still your mother* line will never fly with us, especially me. A mother is a nurturer, a mother is someone who puts her own needs aside to aide to the needs of her children. When the fuck have you done anything like that? The crack meant more to you than the two girls that you fucking held in your own stomach and pushed out. You wanna say you're still someone's mother, tuh. You stopped being my fucking mother the day you let a nigga give you twenty dollars for crack to fuck me."

"What!?"

Tori looked at Eternity who stood on the other side of the room with tears running down her face. Bleek looked at her with a baffled expression on his. This was his first-time hearing of it and suddenly he felt sick to his stomach. He knew that Eternity had it rough growing up, but he didn't know how rough. He walked to her side to let her know that he was there for her. He felt like kicking Machina out of the hospital bed that she was lying in.

"Eternity what are you talking about?" Tori needed answers.

She couldn't recall a time in her memories where her sister was violated. The only thing that came to her mind was the time when she almost was.

"Now you sitting there quiet. You want to shout this mother shit when you are the furthest thing from it. Tori remember the day auntie Nora came and got you to take you to school but I stayed home because momma said that I had a bug?"

Tori shook her head up and down because it was the only memory that she had of Eternity being sick.

When she was younger, she was worried if she would catch the same bug that Eternity had gotten.

"Yeah, that was the morning after she let that nigga have his way with me. I was fucking thirteen years old!" Tori covered her mouth with her hand and let the tears flow down her face.

"The shit happened a year before she tried to let that man touch me?" Tori asked.

"Yeah," Eternity wiped her nose with the back of my hand, "that's why when I came out the room that night and saw that she was trying to sell your body too I had enough and killed that man. She had been selling me for a whole fucking year and I was not about to let her do the same to you."

Eternity turned her attention to her mother, "fuck your apologies."

She walked out of the room with Bleek and Tori following behind her. When she made it into the hall she broke down into tears.

"What the fuck happened?" Sha asked as he watched Bleek embrace Eternity.

"My fucking sister is the strongest bitch I know that's what the fuck happened," Tori said through tears.

"Shhh shhh," Bleek consoled Eternity as he rubbed her back.

His mind was blown, he knew that Eternity had inner demons that she had to vent about before her mother had died but he had no idea that it would be some shit like this. A molester and pedophile were things that he did not take lightly. His nose flared because he wanted to hunt down every single man that put a finger on her and kill them.

He wanted to make their deaths slow. She had been holding in her pain for years and now she was finally letting it out. Years locked away in a cell she still did not get this pain off of her chest.

"I hope she burns in hell…" she cried into Bleek's shoulder.

Her makeup was smearing on his cream-colored hoodie, but he didn't care. His strong hand cupped the back of her head and then massaged her noggin.

"Sis I know you feel better now that the shit is off your chest though and I swear if I never said it before I'ma say it now… thank you for saving me from having to go through that."

Eternity broke her embrace from Bleek and then looked at Tori with her puffy red eyes.

"That's what the fuck I was supposed to do."

"Aight y'all let's go and get some food before we have to catch our flight back home."

Bleek grabbed Eternity's chin and turned her to face him.

"Leave this hurt shit in New York, ma. You went in there and instead of addressing the pain she had put you through she expected instant forgiveness and that shit isn't right."

She dropped her head, allowing her chin to hit her chest and when she did, tears stained the top of her t-shirt. He lifted her head.

"Stop it. Head up baby girl. We about to go back home y'all gone get shit ready for Tori's beauty bar and then we will get our youth center together. You about to be too busy with business to even be phased by this you hear me." He kissed her button nose and then wiped her face clean.

"Damn bro, you be speaking some movie shit word. About to make a real nigga tear up over here."

Sha playfully wiped the side of his eye as if a tear were falling.

"You are an asshole," Tori playfully slapped him in the arm.

He caught her arm.

"You good?"

He didn't know exactly what had transpired in the room, but he could see the hurt in her eyes as well. She shook her head up and down quickly but that wasn't good enough for him.

"Are you good?" he asked again.

This time his face was closer to hers. He wanted her to know that in this kind of situation it was perfectly fine if she wasn't okay. When he saw the tears fill her round orbs, he just embraced her.

"Y'all go ahead and find somewhere near the airport for us to eat at. Text one of us the details, we're right behind you."

Bleek and Eternity shook their head and then made their exit.

"You know you can talk to me about this shit, right?"

Tori had been closed off since they had started dating and he had been trying to get her to open up, but he knew that it would only take time. She shook her head up and down but still didn't speak on what occurred inside of that hospital room.

"Let's go let's go! She's coding."

Tori turned around to see doctors and nurses rushing to the room that her mother was in. She rushed to the doorway with Sha at her side. A doctor ripped her mother's gown open.

"Charge!"

Another doctor placed the paddles onto Machina's chest. Tori watched in shock as her mother's body lifted from the bed in a bolt of energy before flatlining again. Tori turned away because it was too graphic for her to see. She figured that her mother was clinging onto life until she was able to make amends with her girls.

"Let's go... she's been dead to us for a while now." Sha looked at her with uncertainty.

"Are you sure? You don't want to call E and tell her—"

"Absolutely not, like I said she's been dead to us for a while."

She walked away and headed towards the elevators.

"Time of death, sixteen fifty."

Sha shook his head and then jogged lightly in the hall to catch up with Tori.

*C*hapter 10

The nerves was starting to set in, and she knew that it was only because of the grand opening later that night.

"Do you think that we did enough social media promotion?"

"Sis relax I've paid for promotion on Instagram and Facebook in all the surrounding states and Bleek paid them kids to past flyers out up and down Collins Avenue. Tonight, will be a success, okay?"

Eternity had to talk the nerves away from Tori. Both women sat in chairs getting their makeup done by the top makeup artists in the city. Bleek wanted the night to be perfect for them both so he had no limit on what he had spent to ensure that it would be. He stood in the doorway and watched as the two women engaged in conversation.

A smile crept on his face because this is what he had been wanting for years. This lifestyle he had right now is all that he had been needing. A woman at his side with a little family of his own. Tori in a sense was like their child and they both spoiled and looked out for her as if she were. His phone vibrating in his pocket broke him from his stare he had on the ladies. When he took his iPhone out of the pocket of his slacks, he saw that it was Paris calling him.

He sighed and then sent the call to voicemail. She had been calling him nonstop ever since he sent Talia, one of Sha's childhood friends and the woman responsible for cooking up his work, to her home to accompany her to the abortion clinic. Talia assured Bleek that the procedure was done and successful. Once he had that reassurance to him, there was nothing for him and Paris to talk about.

In one night, he had saw her true colors and he told himself that there was nothing that she could say that could make him look at her differently. When his phone vibrated again in his hand, he checked his text messages.

Paris: I never thought that we would get here but it's cool, I guess… The abortion is done

He quickly read over the text and then locked his phone.

"How do I look?"

He jumped at the sound of Eternity's voice. Her eyebrows scrunched in curiosity.

"What's wrong with you?"

"Nothing... what did you say?" he asked as he looked her into her eyes.

"It doesn't even matter. We should be ready in an hour."

She brushed past him to walk away but he grabbed her arm with her passing.

"Stop... your mad and we not about to ignore it," he sighed.

He wasn't the kind of man that was into keeping shit from his lady so, he knew that he had to come clean with this.

"You asked what's wrong with me and I just lied."

He looked into the room and saw that Tori was still getting her makeup done.

"Come."

He pulled Eternity into the nearby bathroom and then closed the door behind them. He leaned up against the bathroom door to brace himself. It wasn't like he cheated or anything, but he knew that the topic of children was a sensitive one for both of them. He leaned up against the door because he was sure that once he had come clean about the situation with Paris that Eternity would try and leave the room.

Whenever they hit a snag in their relationship she would run away, and he hated that shit about her. Bleek ran his hand down his face. He looked at her for a while. Her face was beat to perfection. He didn't mind the makeup artist fee once he saw the outcome. Not yet dressed in her gown she stood in front of him with just her pajama nightgown on.

She wore furry slippers with the toes out that showed off her purple toenail polish. He looked her up and down, from head to toe. She was fucking perfection to him. With her arms crossed over her torso she waited for him to speak.

"The girl I was dealing with, the night I went to break it off I saw that she had a pregnancy test in the garbage." Eternity held onto the side of the sink with one hand and then covered her stomach with the other. *He's about to have a baby...* the thought came to her and instantly she felt sick.

"Fuckkkk why did you have to tell me today of all days Malik. You are going to be a father?"

"No…" he quickly answered, "she told me that she wanted to get an abortion and honestly I didn't agree with it at first. You know me ma, I'm the furthest thing from a fucking dead beat. What's my blood is good forever but then she sat in my face and told me that you had called me last year before Malik died you fucking called me, and she blocked your number. That shit… that shit—"

"It was her that answered your phone that day."

Eternity shook her head from side to side. She remembered the day like it was yesterday.

"I was fresh out of the hospital after the car accident and all I wanted to do was leave. I wanted to come to you and tell you all about Malik being yours. She fucking answered and said that you were busy. My stupid ass thought it was someone from one of your shops."

Bleek listened to her. Had he known that she had called Paris would have been cancelled a long time ago.

He knew it and he was sure that Paris knew it as well and that is why she went ahead and blocked Eternity's number from his phone.

"Yeah, well after she told me that shit, I made sure that she got that abortion. That's some devious toxic shit to do and I'll be damned if I bring life into this world with a female like that."

Eternity listened to him. He was always logical. The weary feeling in her stomach started to subside but of course she still had doubts.

"How do you even know that she got the abortion?" He could sense the skepticism in her tone and that shit ate him up.

Although they weren't together at the time, he was never careless with his dick. Not many females had the pleasure of saying that they felt him, all of him in the natural state without the barrier of latex protection. So, he felt stupid for even letting her be one that was added to his selective list.

"I sent one of my homegirls to go with her. It's done."

Eternity felt a sense of relief. She loved Bleek but she did not know if the strength of her love could bear him being the father to a child that was not hers. She sighed out loud and then clapped her hands.

"Whew, boy you fucking scared me."

She dabbed the corner of her right eye with her finger because she felt the tear about to fall. He looked at her and watched as the uncertainty and fear washed away from her facial expression. It scared him because he wondered if Paris had not gotten the abortion would she had stayed with him. He wanted to ask her badly, but he feared her response, so he didn't. Him asking only would have ended in an unnecessary argument because there was no baby to even be discussing.

"Sorry I had to tell you today. I just saw the annoyance on your face when I said nothing."

"It's because I know you Malik. I knew something was bothering you."

"Come here."

She walked over to him and stood in his embrace.

"My makeup is gonna be on your dress shirt."

Bleek looked down at her and then kissed her forehead.

"I don't give a fuck. I have another one upstairs."

"You love me enough to fuck up this expensive ass Armani shirt?"

"Eternity, I love you more than I love myself."

There was no game in his statement, he meant that shit. She rolled her eyes upward so that she could look him in his face.

"I know."

There was no doubt in her tone. Over the years he had shown just how much he had loved her and now, finally she was reciprocating it the way she should have always been.

Knock, Knock

"Y'all get y'all asses out the bathroom. Find another day to do your freaky shit. Today is MY day."

Bleek and Eternity chuckled at the sound of Tori's voice on the other side of the door. They had yet to have sex since they had gotten back together but the tension between them was heavy. Bleek was patient, he moved at her pace and the waiting game only made things better for him. He knew that when he entered her again that it would be the best she had ever gotten because he would be backed up.

"Nobody is doing anything nasty," Eternity yelled back.

"Yeah, whatever just get the fuck out of the bathroom."

Eternity rolled her eyes and then broke her embrace with Bleek. He leaned off of the bathroom door, turned around and opened it. Tori stood in front of him in a robe with a royal blue dramatic beat applied to her face.

"You look gorgeous sis."

He moved a curl from out of her face as he gave the compliment.

"Uh uh, don't touch nothing with those fingers I don't know where the fuck they been."

Both Bleek and Eternity laughed.

"Man, let me go and change this shirt. Y'all get y'all asses together the van will be here in about twenty minutes. Did Sha make it here yet?" Bleek asked Tori as he walked past her.

"Yeah, his ass is in the kitchen like there isn't food at the shop. He gets on my damn nerve."

"That boy can fucking eat," Bleek chuckled, "aight y'all twenty fucking minutes. Let's go."

Bleek walked past Tori and made his way upstairs. While walking up the stairs one of his guards called for his attention.

"Hey boss."

Bleek turned around and then stood on the stairs.

"Yeah, what's up."

"Okay so we have guards at the shop, and we have a car following behind you guys en route there. Is there anything else that you need?"

Bleek stood for a moment to think. He had taken the extra precautions with security since the sit down with Manny. It was clear that Chiva Blanca was not going to back down, so he had to make sure that his family was good.

"I think that's good. Were we able to get the van that was bulletproof?"

"Yes boss, the windows and doors on the van is proofed."

"Aight that's it then."

Bleek turned around and then walked up the stairs. He looked in the mirror at the makeup that stained his white dress shirt and then he unbuttoned it. His suit jacket was already downstairs. He took off his cufflinks and then placed them onto the dresser. After grabbing another white, pressed dress shirt out of his closet he started to dress in it.

"Leave it off…"

Bleek turned around to see Eternity behind him. His room doors were now closed and the nightgown she was wearing moments ago was off. Under the gown she only wore a black lace bra and panty set.

"E, what you on?" he asked with a raised eyebrow.

"I want it."

He smirked because he knew that sooner than later that she would cave. He respected her form of celibacy, but it was damn hard for him.

"Ma, we have ten minutes before the van gets here."

"I can cum in five."

Damn, he thought as he bit his bottom lip. He loved when she talked sexy to him. He wanted it just as bad as she did, but he preferred to make her wait. When he touched her again, he didn't want it to be a rush job.

"When I get that again there will be no time limit on me. Put ya dress on ma. When we get home tonight it's all yours."

She pouted but did as she was told. While she went to the closet to put on her gown, he changed his shirt and then put his new cufflinks onto his shirt.

"Mr. Browne the ride is here."

Bleek walked over to his room door and then pulled it open.

"Okay thank you, we'll be right down."

He closed the room door back and when he turned around Eternity stood in front of him in her gown. Her short hair was in finger waves. The yellow colored dress she wore hugged her curves. With a slit on the right side it showed off her thick thigh when she walked.

"Yeah I already see how tonight about to go."

Bleek opened the top drawer to his dresser and then grabbed his gun out.

"Malikkkkkk" Eternity screeched, "you know damn well everyone coming knows better," she giggled.

"Well, just in a case a nigga plan on losing his mind, I'm with whatever." He pressed the eject button on the clip, checked to make sure that it was full and then he inserted the clip back into the gun.

After cocking the gun back to load a bullet into the chamber he put the gun into his back waistband.

"Come on." He put his hand on the lower of her back as he led the way down the stairs. He grabbed his suit jacket off the banister of the stairs and then put it on.

"Well okay y'all look cuteeee" Eternity said cheerfully once she saw Tori and Sha matching. His handkerchief that stuck out of his suit jacket matched the same color blue of her gown. She watched as Sha pulled at the neck of his shirt.

"I fucking feel stuffed."

Bleek lightly chuckled to himself because he knew that his friend was as hood as they came. His ass would wear a pair of jeans and t shirt for every occasion. He knew that the only reason that Sha was dressed up was because Tori made it mandatory. When promoting the event, she made sure to heavily express the fact that everyone in attendance had to be in formal attire. Her place of business was a classy one and she wanted to make that clear with the grand opening.

One of the bodyguards held the front door open. A black tinted Mercedes Benz van waited at the bottom of the stairs.

"You ready?" Bleek asked the ladies as they entered the van.

"Hell yeah," they said in unison.

Both Sha and Bleek smiled, it was something about smiles on the faces of those two Washington ladies that always placed a smile on theirs. It was because of the hardships they had gotten over together. All they had was each other, they didn't need any fair-weather friends that'll up and leave when the clouds got stormy. Na, they had each other and no matter the weather they was always there for one another.

Chapter 11

The beauty bar had a line that extended all the way to the end of the block.

"Do you see all of these people!"

The excitement in Tori's voice made everyone smile. When the van stopped, she gathered the train to her dress in her hand. Sha exited the car first and then he held his hand out for her to exit. When she did, she saw that everyone started to clap. She smiled and waved. Some of the people were workers that helped pull this project together and others she didn't notice at all. She could tell that there were a couple of stars in attendance just by the facial expressions on those surrounding them.

A huge silver ribbon was tied to the doors of the establishment. Through the glass doors she could see the hostesses in there preparing themselves to serve champagne and appetizers. Bleek exited the van next and then helped Eternity out. She looked out to the crowd and then spit formed in her throat when her brown eyes met with his gray ones.

Turning her attention towards her sister she tried to shake the bubbly feeling she had in her stomach. Her palms got sweaty, so she rubbed them together to try and calm her nerves.

"You aight?" Bleek asked.

"Yeah, I'm good."

She walked over to her sister's side just as the event coordinator was handing her a mic.

"Thank you everyone for coming out. I wanted to start with that. Opening my own business has always been a dream of mine," Tori looked to Eternity, "it had always been a dream for my sister and me. This beauty bar is special to me. My family and myself worked day in and day out to get this place together, this is more than just a hair salon. It's an escape for the working woman that just needs some inner peace, it's that therapy session, it's not just somewhere you go for your hair, we do massages, nails, toes, facials and waxes, it's a beauty bar and I am excited to be sharing my little slice of peace with you all."

Everyone started to clap after Tori's speech.

"Should I cut this ribbon now?"

"Yes," the crowd said in unison.

The event coordinator handed Tori a giant pair of bedazzled scissors.

"Come on sis help me."

Eternity smiled. She was watching her baby sister's dreams come true and she was blessed just to be included in the accomplishment.

"Baby girl this is your moment. You do that shit." Tori cheesed, showing off her pearly whites. She opened the scissors and then cut the ribbon.

"Welcome to Nalah's Color Box!" she yelled into the microphone after cutting the ribbon.

Everyone cheered and then followed behind Tori into the shop. R&B music played lightly throughout the space and as Tori watched the crowed fill the inside of her establishment she smiled. Everyone came dressed appropriately. Bleek and Sha walked off to mingle with the guest. Being big names in the streets of Miami a lot of people in attendance knew who they were.

"How does this feel Tori Tee?" Eternity asked.

"It feels fucking amaz— is that Prince?" she asked when she saw a man in a teal suit walk through the door.

"Yup, I spotted his ass outside on the line."

"Mmmm… welp my sister let me go and enjoy the most out of my night before Bleek catches a body in here."

Tori tapped her sister's shoulder before walking away to greet her many future possible customers. Eternity looked around to try and find a place to go. She could see Prince walking in her direction out the corner of her eye. *What the fuck is he doing here?* Instantly she thought about the paid promotion she had done on the shop's Instagram account. She listed every state, she wanted her sister to get all of the exposure that she could. With Prince walking in her direction she instantly regretted doing so. *Fuck, fuck, fuck.* She scanned the room for Bleek but did not see him.

When she looked at the front door, she started to walk quickly towards the man that had just walked in.

"Man-Man come on, let's go this way."

"Well hello to you too, where da hell we going?"

"Away from the crowd."

She drug him towards the back of the shop near Tori's office.

"What are you doing here?" she asked.

"I came to speak to Tori. I saw this damn mini commercial on Instagram and… I just knew this was probably the only shot I had at speaking with her."

Tori looked over Man-Man's shoulder and saw that Prince was looking around for her.

"Have you even tried calling her? You thought coming here would do what?"

Man-Man unbuttoned the top button of his dress shirt. The veins in his neck flexed as he ground his teeth together. The ink that covered his neck popped out in frustration.

"Mayne… no disrespect but—"

"As soon as you say the word, *but* a disrespectful statement will soon follow."

Eternity crossed her arms over her breast with a raised eyebrow. She was in go mode and the annoyance that she had with the man that was standing in front of her could not be hidden. He had hurt her baby sister and even after the hurt he had no intentions on fixing that pain until now. *A little too fucking late,* she thought as she looked over his shoulder at Tori and Sha smiling and talking with two of the guest in attendance. She smiled slightly when she noticed Bleek walk over.

Man-Man turned around and saw the same that Eternity had seen. He had fucked up, slipped up and let another nigga get close to what he thought was his.

"Not the place or time."

Bleek wasn't into a greeting. To him, wanting to mend anything with Tori at her grand opening was some selfish shit. The day was hers and anyone who was coming on some bullshit was a problem to him.

Man-Man looked from Eternity to Bleek. He was irritated with them both for trying to tell him when the right or wrong time was to get some shit off his chest.

As he looked over Bleek's shoulder and saw the smile on Tori's face he bit his bottom lip. Pure happiness coated her profile and he knew that she deserved it. Within the past year she had suffered so much pain.

"Look, y'all right aight… I just want her to know that nobody moved on with fucking Nova and to answer your question Eternity, hell yeah, I've been calling. She don't answer. She even blocked me on social media. I'm sure you told her that a woman answered my phone the day you called. She was helping me move. When Tori left, I couldn't live in that fucking house anymore. I had a failed marriage, loss a daughter and loss the love of my life all while living in that fucking house."

Man-Man stopped speaking because he felt like he was losing the self-control that he had gathered before walking into the shop.

"It's no need to even let her know the shit. She look happy mayne."

He watched from afar as Sha pushed a piece of hair out of Tori's face. He remembered Sha from when Bleek had come to Chattanooga. Jealousy started to bubble in him, but he let it subside because the man was responsible for getting him to the hospital alive the night he had been shot.

"She look so fucking happy mayne."

He shook his head from side to side. Before his sights turned from looking her way, she locked eyes with him. For a moment they stared at one another. He was hopeful that she would at least come over to speak with him but when she turned her head and then finished engaging in the conversation that she was having, he chuckled and then turned away from her.

He had to let her go. She was gone and he knew that the reason for it was all his fault. *I fucked that shit up,* he thought. He sighed and then pulled himself together. He was losing his shit in front of Bleek and Eternity and that was unlike him. He knew that when he went back home that he would have to continue with what he had been doing over the past months, drowning himself in his work. He turned to walk away.

"Man-Man," Eternity called out.

He turned around to look her way.

"You taught her how to be how she is now you know? Don't be too hard on yourself. Before my sister met you, she didn't know how to love someone properly. Now, I don't know if she's in love, but I can tell you that this is the happiest I have ever seen her."

Man-Man shook his head up and down. Although he was jealous, he would rather see her happy even if it meant not being with him. He walked away and then made his exit. His trip to Miami wasn't a total waste, at least he was able to see her again. He felt better inside knowing that she was good.

"Nigga was really about to try and ruin her day for real..."

Eternity still had an attitude. She understood where he was coming from but to her his ass could have waited until the night was over.

"There you are, were you running away from me." The sound of Prince's voice caused her to look up and caused Bleek to turn around. The smile on his face was charming which pissed Bleek off.

"Oh no, I wasn't I was going to say hello I'm just busy with making sure that everything is running smoothly."

Bleek looked over his shoulder at Eternity. He was waiting on her to introduce him.

"Ah hem," he cleared his throat.

"Malik this is Prince, Prince this is Malik... my boyfriend."

Prince's eyebrows raised.

"Ohhh boyfriend... mmm okay. How you doing man?"

Prince held his hand out for a shake and Bleek looked at it. The way he gave that *mmm okay* comment didn't sit well with him.

"Eternity is this the same Prince that you was just fucking with?"

He never took his eyes off of the man standing in front of him. When Prince realized that Bleek was not going to shake his hand he pulled his hand back in and then placed it into his pocket.

"Yeah..." her voice was low.

"You invited him?"

He needed to know what type of shit she was on. That little *mmm okay* comment made him being there seem funny.

"No, I didn't."

"Cool. What you doing here my guy?"

The tension between the two men could be felt by Eternity. Prince chuckled because he could see that the man in front of him was insecure. He knew that he must have heard of him.

"The shade you're giving this way isn't needed but it's coo that just means that you have heard of me yet... I've heard nothing of you."
Prince looked over Bleek's shoulder and made eye contact with Eternity.

"You said you were leaving to find your peace or whatever not another nigga."
He completely ignored Bleek's question.

"Well, what I said wa—"

"What you said don't even matter. It was said and you left so again, what you doing here?" Bleek cut off Eternity and directed his last question towards Prince.

He was losing his patience and Eternity knew it. She knew that once his patience was gone that bullets would soon follow.

"I saw about the grand opening on social media and thought that I would come support a *friend*, that's it, that's all."

"Cool, she saw you come show your support now you can leave."

"I'll leave when she tells me to. Matter fact you should walk away and let us have a private conversation." Prince put his hand on Bleek's shoulder and went to brush past him to get to Eternity.

In one swift movement Bleek pushed Prince up against the wall and then came off the hip with his gun. Discreetly he pushed the metal nose into Prince's side.

"Didn't your arm just fucking heal? You wanna be out the game again for good from a bullet wound?" Bleek knew exactly who he was when he had first saw him. He was a sports watcher. He just never thought that Eternity's Prince was the same Prince that belonged to the Atlanta Falcons.

"Look man—"

"Look what?"

Bleek dug the gun into his side more. Eternity watched on with wide eyes.

Everyone else was so preoccupied with the gathering that no one noticed the scene that Bleek was putting on in the back corner of the shop.

"Fuck you put ya hand on me for? I said what I said, and I meant it. You came to show your support, now get the fuck out of here before I make Florida your resting place."

Bleek removed the gun from Prince's side and then took two steps back to give the man his space. With nothing else to say Prince just looked at Bleek and then Eternity before he left. Eternity let out the breath she had been holding in since Bleek had come off the hip with his gun.

After tucking the gun back into his waist, he turned to face her.

"I really didn't invite him."

She didn't know what was going through his mind, but she could see the anger in his bushy eyebrows.

"I believe you. What I don't believe is that nigga thinking he was just about to bitch me."

Eternity smirked because Bleek was showing off his masculine side.

"That was sexy you know," she complimented.

"What?"

"All that *get the fuck outta here before I make Florida your resting place,*" she put on deep voice as she mimicked him.

"Shut the fuck up," he let out a husky laugh.

He put his hand on the lower of her back and then led them to the crowd towards Tori and Sha.

They were in the middle of posing for pictures when one of the guards walked up to Bleek and then whispered in his ear.

"Mr. Browne you have someone outside for you."

"Tell them to get checked with security and then come in."

"They insisted on you coming outside."

Bleek sucked his teeth and then flared his spade shaped nose in annoyance.

"Let that nigga know that if he don't bring his ass inside then there is nothing to talk about."

"It's a woman she says her name is Chiva Blanca."

Bleek's eyes opened wide. He kissed Eternity on the side of the head and then nodded for Sha to follow him out.

"Let everyone know that there is a threat outside."

The guard shook his head up and down as he spoke into a mic that was on the collar of his dress shirt. Eternity grabbed Bleek's hand before he could walk away.

"What's going on?" she asked.

"Stay inside I don't care what you hear outside you hear me."

A sadness took over her orbs as she looked at him.

"Do you hear me?" he asked again.

"Yeah, yeah I hear you."

He kissed her lips and to her the kiss felt final. It sent a chill down her spine that worried her.

Tori was too preoccupied with entertaining the guest to notice the mayhem that was about to occur. Eternity picked up the necklace that rested on her neck and then kissed the tiny gold baby's feet. *Watch over daddy Lik,* she thought as she watched Bleek walk out of the door.

"Where the fuck did she go?"

Bleek's head was on a swivel as soon as he made it outside.

"She was just right here," the guard said as he looked up and down the block.

"Why didn't you have someone stand the fuck out here with her."

He was pissed because this was his one opportunity to put whatever beef it was that the woman named Chiva Blanca had with him to rest but it slipped out of his grasp. He slapped his security detail upside the head.

"How the fuck did you let her get away."

The man rubbed the back of his bald head from the slap.

"I'm sorry boss."

"What the fuck did she look like?" Bleek asked.

"Like a Mexican lady. She was gorgeous."

"She was gorgeous," Bleek mocked the man, "you worried about this bitch's looks when she wants to fucking kill me. You know how I want her to look? Huh?"

"Umm—"

"I want her to look fucking dead!" Bleek cut the man off, "fuckkkk!" he roared in frustration.

People passing by looked at him like he was crazy, but he didn't care.

"Bro chill out we gone get this bitch."

"I just want to know what the fuck her beef is with me!"

"At this point bro, it don't even matter. She trynna get at you so we gotta get at her first. We gone get her." Sha reassured.

Bleek shook his head up and down but inside he was seething. He hated not being in the front of a problem. He hated that he felt like he had to look over his shoulder every single time that he did something.

"Aight, you right," he agreed with Sha.

Bleek stared at the guard he had on payroll as he and Sha made their way back into the salon.

"Fucking idiot," he mumbled under his breath before they walked in.

***

"Why do you always get this drunk?" Eternity chuckled to Tori as Sha helped her out of the salon.

"You... you be the drunk one."

Tori stopped talking to hiccup.

"Bitch did you just hiccup like them drunk ass cartoon characters."

Eternity laughed loudly. The salon was empty, and the night was a success. Tori's assistant was in attendance and had booked women for appointments in the coming weeks. With every appointment booked, a deposit was mandatory so not only did Tori end her night drunk as hell, but she made a little bag as well.

"Pick up her dress, it's dragging all over the floor," Eternity yelled.

"Ma, you drunk as fuck too all this yelling you doing."

"WHO ME?" Eternity giggled, "Oh shit I was loud as fuck."

"See told you sis you drunk lika me. Bayyyybeeeee pick my dress up you know how much you paid for this shit."

Sha shook his head as he picked up the train to Tori's dress and then threw it over his shoulder before swooping her into his arms.

"Wowwww this boy strong. Emily… lock this bitch up when we leave."

Tori's assistant shook her head and then started to gather her personal items so that she could leave right behind them. When the group of four made it outside the breeze caused Eternity to cover her arms immediately. Bleek took off his jacket and then wrapped it around her shoulders. They walked to the van that was waiting on them.

Two guards followed behind them.

"We will be in the car behind you," the same guard from earlier said to Bleek.

He didn't even acknowledge the man with a verbal response because he was still pissed off at what had occurred earlier in the night. Once everyone was inside of the van the driver closed the door and then went to get in the driver's seat.

"Ughhh my stomach is killing me," Tori groaned.

"Well nobody told your ass to eat strawberries, have all that sweet shit, drink champagne and then turn around and drink fucking henny. You thought you was a big dog."

"Howlllll I am the big dog."

"Then why the fuck did you just make a damn wolf noise?" Eternity asked.

Everyone in the van laughed.

"Ya drunk ass is embarrassing," Sha said as he shook his head.

"No what's embarrassing is the way my sad ass ex looked tonight."

"What?" Sha asked.

Eternity and Bleek looked away from them.

"What the fuck is she talkin—"

Sha stopped speaking when the van stopped short causing everyone's body to jerk towards the front of the van.

"What the fuck is going on?" Bleek asked the driver.

"Sir, there is a group of three men standing in the middle of the street."

Bleek caught a hallow feeling in the pit of his stomach.

"Run them over."

"Sir what?"

"Run them the fuck ov—"

Before Bleek could finish his statement the sound of gun fire erupted.

Boom... Ping... Boom Boom... Ping Ping

The sound of gunfire and the bullets hitting the metal of the van could be heard.

"Fucking drive!"

Bleek was happy in the moment that he had decided for them to take the van that was bullet proofed.

"Are we being fucking shot at?" Eternity screamed out as the van wildly drove down the street.

"One of tires is out," the driver yelled to the back.

"I don't give a fuck if you gotta break the rims on this bitch do not fucking pull over. Are they following us?" The driver looked into the side mirrors and saw that the car behind them was having a standoff with the three men that were in the middle of the street.

"No, the car behind us is taking care of them."

"That shit was a close—" Tori threw up in Sha's lap before she could finish her statement.

"Oh, hell no ewww ewww I can't see fucking thro—"

Eternity turned to the side and then threw up on the floor of the van.

"What kind of nasty shit is this!" Sha yelled. Bleek just shook his head as he rubbed Eternity's back.

"No really… what kind of nasty shit is this? I have warm throw up and a passed out drunk ass rookie in my lap, I'm looking at throw up on the floor. We just got fucking shot at and her bitch ass ex came lurking around tonight. I need a fucking blunt."

Bleek reached into the pocket of his dress shirt and then pulled a neatly wrapped blunt from it.

"Oh, hell yeah," Sha said with a smile once he saw it, "send that."

Bleek leaned up in his chair to hand Sha the blunt but when the van drove over a bump Bleek dropped the blunt.

"Are you fucking kidding me? The shit just had to fall in the throw up. Yo fuck this night, dead ass."

Bleek laughed as Sha sucked his teeth. The night had been an eventful one. Bleek knew that he would have to get his loved ones out of the state for a bit. Things with Chiva Blanca was too hot. He knew that going to D.R was an option, but he needed to have a talk with his brother because if he was coming then he was bringing Tori, Eternity and Sha with him. He didn't know how Ty would feel having Tori or Eternity around after all of these years.

*C*hapter 12

Sleep didn't come easy to Bleek the night before. Too much had happened and too quickly for him to rest easy. He beefed up on the security detail on his estate. He always had guards and to him he didn't really need them until now. Not only was this woman trying to take his life from him, but she had a way of playing mind games along with it. He really wished that he knew what her motive was. At least then he could understand the situation a little better. If he hated anything in life it was being put in a situation that he did not understand.

It was three in the morning and he was pacing his family room on the first floor. Eternity was knocked out in his bed and Sha had stayed the night and was with Tori in hers.

"Sir you can sleep we have the perimeter covered. You can get some rest."

One of his many guards stood in the doorway of the room.

"Na, I'm good. You have men surrounding the home and the gate to the estate as well?"

"Yes sir. We loss two great men last night, I don't intend on losing anymore."

Bleek nodded his head. His security detail was ex-military and law enforcement men and he only hired men that was a great shot, just as him.

"Go ahead, I'm good here."

Bleek wanted his privacy.

He stood facing the flames of the fireplace. Every bad deed he had ever done played in his mind. *This bitch said it was personal,* he thought to himself. He was certain that when he handled business that he cut all loose ends to avoid situations like this yet, he was caught up in one. He took his cellphone out of the pocket of his pajama pants and then placed a FaceTime call to Ty.

He knew that his brother would be up because for years Ty always woke up around three am. It was an uneasy part of the early morning that always woke him out of his slumber. On the second ring he answered. Bleek saw that he was standing in his kitchen in front of the stove. The phone was propped up on something.

"You cooking nigga?"

"Hell yeah, I send the chef home at a certain time and I woke up with my stomach growling and shit. This pregnant shit got me getting all the cravings. Toya's ass is in here knocked out drooling and here I am making a fucking pastrami egg and cheese sandwich."

Bleek chuckled, *"that pregnant shit be wild."*

"The fuck you doing up nigga?" Ty asked.

"Man... it's a lot going on."

"Catch me up, I'm here."

Bleek sat on the couch in the room and then revealed the night before to Ty. He also told him of his son that had died and the relationship he now shared with Eternity.

"Well damn, you had one hell of a year," was the only thing that came out of Ty's mouth once Bleek finished speaking.

He had finished his sandwich and was now laid across the couch in his own living room.

"Yeah but my biggest problem right now is this Chiva Blanca bitch. I didn't get this woman back into my life to have to let her go to save her. I'm not with that shit."

Bleek swiped his hand over his face in stress.

"Y'all need to get low for a little minute, at least until you get to the bottom of this shit. You and your lady can come out here."

Ty wasn't a fan of Eternity, but he loved his brother and the Dominican army that rested on his estate lived to protect him and his family. He knew that Bleek had his own security and to him that was cool, but those men wasn't born to protect Bleek.

For as long as the Ruiz Dynasty has been a thing, Dominican men prepped themselves to be a part of its protection army.

"I appreciate the offer bro, but my family now consist of her sister too. Tori is my sister just how you are my brother and you remember my homebody Sha right? That's his lady. Does this invitation extend to them as well?"

Ty gritted his teeth.

"Yeah, you my brother and your safety is my concern, I understand that you have your own family and because you are my brother their safety is my concern too. I'll talk to Toya in the morning to put her up on game. If you don't hear from me in the morning that mean she probably slit my throat," Ty nervously chuckled as he massaged his own neck, *"but seriously bro. It's not a problem ever since she got pregnant with our son she could care less about the extra shit. If staying in this house makes you uncomfortable y'all are welcome to stay in the extra house on the land down the road. Magdala retired earlier this year so the house she had is empty. It's a three-bedroom, three bath. It should be suitable for y'all."*

Bleek shook his head up and down as he listened.

"Damn when the fuck did your nanny retire? I thought she would have died working for y'all."

Ty chuckled, *"I did too but I saw the tired shit in her eyes dealing with the girls is a lot and she's an older woman you know. I still pay her as if she's here. She sends us post cards of everywhere she visits. She always talked about traveling."*

Ty tapped his phone screen to see the time and saw that it was now five in the morning.

"Aight I gotta get back in the bed before Paige come in the room complaining about Lily being up. Book y'all tickets we here."

"We might just take my jet. I don't feel like dealing with the public right now. It's like I don't know who to trust," Bleek admitted.

"Understandable, get some rest you look tired as fuck." Ty said as he looked at this brother.

"Night bro," Bleek said.

"Shitttt it's morning now," Ty chuckled, *"later."*

After Ty hung up, Bleek locked his phone and then dropped it onto his chest. He laid on his sofa with his arms behind his head. As soon as he closed his eyes Eternity's sweet voice spoke.

"There you are."

He opened his eyes and looked up at the ceiling.

"Here I am."

When she rounded the couch, he leaned up. She sat in the spot and got comfortable before he laid down into her lap. Her hand rubbed over his hair. In an up and down motion her fingers rose and then fell over his deep waves.

"What's on your mind boo?" She asked.

He sighed and it felt like he was releasing the weight of the world off his chest.

"If something would have happened to one of y'all last night—"

"But it didn't."

"But it could have."

"You're worrying about the negative, think about the positive of the situation. Those bullets didn't start until we were protected in that vehicle. They could have started while we was walking. We could have all been shot but we weren't, thank God."

Bleek listened to her. This new optimistic version of her is one he still had to get used to. The Eternity he was used to was one that always spoke on the negative side of things. It was refreshing getting this edition of her.

"I arranged for us to go to D.R for a little bit. At least until shit cools down."

"Is this like a vacation? Or did you make this arrangement with your *family*?"
She could hear the uncertainty in her tone.

"I spoke with Ty and *all of us* are going."

He knew that she would be uncomfortable with the arrangement because it was no secret that she wasn't Ty's favorite person and with Tori's and Ty's brief history she knew that this situation could get messy.

"I don't think I'm comfortable with that."

"Do you trust me?"

She looked down into his brown eyes.

"Of course, I do," she answered.

"We gone be good aight?"

"Okay…"

She knew that she could put her ill feelings aside for their safety, but she wasn't sure if Tori could do the same.

***

"You want me to go fucking where?"

Tori sucked her teeth as she looked at Eternity and Bleek standing at the foot of her bed. She still felt sick from the night before.

"I'm not fucking going to D.R to be around that nigga and his fucking *wife*."

Bleek and Eternity shook their head at Tori's stubbornness. Sha was coming out of the bathroom from brushing his teeth.

"What the fuck is the problem with going?" He was confused.

"I used to talk to Ty. It's a long story," Tori said nonchalantly.

"Well damn, you got more niggas than fucking Wu-tang. It was the nigga at the mall, your fucking ex popping out to your events and now you saying you used to fuck with his mans?"

"More niggas than Wu-tang?" Eternity questioned as she laughed at Sha's statement.

Everyone in the room shared a laugh.

"Seriously y'all I'm not going. Plus, after the shooting down the block from the shop I need to watch out for my business."

"Tori why the fuck do you think that this is up for debate. This bitch is not gonna stop until she kills me or someone that I love. With me, I know you gone be safe." Bleek was losing patience with trying to explain the severity of the danger that they now all was in.

"Bro, she gone be good with me. I ain't into the fashion of being around *another* ex of hers," Sha said as he cut eyes at Tori.

She rolled her eyes at him and then clapped her hands.

"So, it's settled. We'll be here. To make you feel better we will even stay at the house okay?"

"Whatever," Bleek said before turning to leave the room.

"Enjoy your vacation," she called out to him and her sister once Eternity started to follow behind them.

***

The hot beaming sun is something that Bleek would never get used to. He used the back of his hand to wipe the sweat from his forehead. *I fucking hate it here.* He had a love, hate relationship with the island. The weather was on the frown upon side, but he always loved the time he spent with Ty and Toya. Eternity looked out of the tinted window of the truck as the verdant trees passed her by.

She shook her leg involuntarily because her nerves was bad. Once Bleek placed his hand on her knee she stopped.

"Calm down, aight."

She gave no response she just looked at him with a weak smile. She didn't even know why her nerves was so bad. She could careless how Ty felt about her, but she knew that his feelings was a heavy influence on Bleek.

A Love Affair for Eternity BOOK 4: THE FINALE

In the beginning on their love story she didn't even care what Bleek thought of her because she was just living life and having fun. With over ten years later from the start of them she cared about what he thought heavily. When they pulled up to the enormous black gate, Eternity looked at the army of Dominican men that was scattered out on the lawn.

"This is how he lives?"

"Shit if I was living this way, I wouldn't have to worry about some damn Chiva Blanca," Bleek mumbled.

As their car pulled up, Eternity saw two little girls playing on the front yard. They were both clothed in floral print dresses. A smile crept onto Eternity's face as she watched the two little girls play their own made up version of freeze tag. It was the curly locks, moisturized bronze skin and green eyes for her. The girls were stunning. When the driver pulled and opened the door for her and Bleek, the two girls looked in their direction.

"Uncle Leeeekkkkk," they both squealed as they ran full speed towards him.

Bleek used both of his arms to scoop the girls into his hold. The older one of the two wrapped her arms around his neck and then laid on his chest.

"Can y'all say hi to my girlfriend? Her name is Eternity."

"Hi," the youngest one showed off her toothless smile and then waved.

"Paige," Bleek shook his arm with the older child in it, "say hi."

"Mmmm," she groaned as she looked away with an attitude.

"Lily is the friendly one," he said with a smile before trying to put the girls down.

Lily got down without a struggle while Paige held onto his neck tighter.

"Paige, uncle will sneak you some cookies later if you go and play with your sister now."

She looked into his face and then smiled brightly.

"Pinky promise?" She held her small pinky up, so he wrapped his pinky around hers.

"Pinky promise," he ensured.

He then put her down and then turned to face Eternity. He looked at the smile on her face.

"What?" He asked.

"I never saw the kid side to you."

He could sense the sadness in her tone. He knew that she was wondering how he would have been with their son. Those thoughts crossed his mind every single time he was around his nieces.

"Come on."

He led the way up the stairs and into the house. He knew that the door had to be open because the girls were playing outside.

"Yooooooo," he called out.

"Yerrrrrrr."

A male's voice from upstairs called out.

"Y'all are so New York," Eternity said with a chuckle.

She looked at the stairs and saw Ty coming down them. When he reached the bottom, he shook hands with Bleek like only gangsters could.

"Ghetto ghetto," he greeted Eternity.

"Ty that lies," she greeted him back.

"Y'all gone dead this shit right now. It's been years and we're too old for the shit."

Both Ty and Eternity looked at Bleek.

"Fine," they said in unison.

Bleek shook his head because he was sure that Eternity and Ty would be at each other's throat again before they left.

"Where sis at?" He asked.

"She'll be down in a min morning sickness fucked with her all morning she just now getting it together from then. Where's the rest of your company?"

Ty looked at the open door behind Bleek and only saw his daughters playing on the lawn.

"They decided not to come. Tori gotta handle business with the shop, the shooting outside of it wasn't a good look. So, where's the key to the house down the road?"

"Y'all not gonna stay here? I mean like the extra people didn't come so is the crib needed?"

Bleek already knew that Eternity was uncomfortable around Ty. She had been for years and he always made sure to keep the two out of the same room for that reason.

"Yeah it's needed. Where's the key?"

Ty rounded the stairs' banister and then made his way to the kitchen in the back. Both Bleek and Eternity followed. Ty dug around inside one of the kitchen drawers and then pulled a set of keys out.

"Here," he tossed them Bleek's way and he caught them, "it should be clean because I was still sending the cleaning lady down there."

"TYSHAWN!"

Ty rolled his eyes.

"She been mean as hell bro. I just need her to give me my son and that's it," he whispered, "yeah ma!" He yelled.

"I can't find my slippers!"

"Girl as much as I pay muthafuckas to mop and buff these floors you don't need them. Plus, you clumsy as hell I don't need you slipping down the stairs."

There was a moment of silence.

"Fuck you," Toya yelled out.

Bleek and Eternity laughed.

"Y'all like an old ass married couple now," Bleek said in a chuckle.

"Bro we been this way. Where y'all luggage?"

"Still in the truck. It didn't even make sense to take it out when I'ma have us driven down the road to the other crib."

"Aight cool."

"So, I have to really walk around these cold ass floors barefooted?"

Everyone turned their attention to the voice that had just entered the room. Toya stood in front of them in a safari printed sun dress with swollen bare feet beneath her.

"Damn sis you look like my nephew about to fall out ya ass any minute."

Eternity slapped Bleek on the shoulder.

"Fuck you fuck boy," Toya said as she playfully stuck up her middle finger.

"I'm playing. You know I'm playing. Sis this is my lady Eternity, E this is my sis Toya."

Eternity cringed at her name, to her it was too close to her sister's name. All of this time she only heard of *Ty's wife*. She never had a name or face to place to the title. Eternity was the kind of woman that gave compliments when they were due, so she had to give it to Toya, she was naturally stunning. Even standing in front of her with a spread nose, swollen feet and rounded belly, Eternity saw that she was remarkable.

Both women lightly smiled at one another but didn't say much.

"Aight, well we about to go down the block."

"You like *down the block* like we're back home or something. Are y'all staying in the guest house?" Toya asked.

"Yup," Bleek answered.

"Well take some towels and rags out the closet upstairs cause ain't none down there."

"I packed us some," Eternity said with a smile.

"That's what I'm talking about girl. I pack us towels and rags whenever we travel," Toya said with a chuckle, "where's the other two people that were supposed to come."

"They decided to stay, they had some business to handle," Eternity answered before Bleek could.

"Oh okay, well there's more than enough space for just y'all two up the road. Are y'all coming back for dinner tonight?"

"You cooking?" Bleek asked with a raised eyebrow.

"Hell no, you see this belly. My mom is gonna come over with Tony. She's cooking."

"Aight cool," Bleek said and then licked his lips. He had to give to Toya's mother she knew how to throw down in the kitchen.

"See y'all later," Toya said when Bleek and Eternity got up to exit.

ＣＣhapter 13

Bleek turned the key into the door and then held it open for Eternity. He then picked up their two suitcases and drug them across the threshold of the house. The home was no mansion like Ty's house, but it was more so of a vacation home. It was ranch styled and spacious. Colors of white, mint green and yellow dressed the rooms in the quarters.

"This is fucking nice," Eternity said as she pulled back the sheer curtains to the windows on the back patio.

Water rested a few feet up and with the sun setting it looked amazing. She felt the warmth of Bleek's body standing behind her, so she leaned back into his chest. He kissed the side of her head.

"If you don't want to go back down the block for dinner we don't have to."

"No, it's fine, I really felt okay being there. What you said is right. There's no real beef between Ty and me. My sister is happy where she is, and he is damn sure happy where he is. And we are happy, that's all that matters." Bleek sighed, a sense of relief washed over him.

He kissed her head once more.

"Come on lets unpack."

He grabbed her hand and then led the way to the master bedroom. When he pushed the door open, he saw rose petals placed onto the bed into heart shaped form.

"Ohhh Malik this is gorgeous!" Eternity squealed into excitement.

"Hell yeah, it is."

It was a shock to him too. He knew that Ty had to have been the one to have the extra décor arranged.

"You must be trynna get some tonight."

Eternity smirked.

"You want some?"

She sat onto the bed and then parted her thick thighs.

"Well shit, hell yeah."

Bleek pulled his shirt over his head. He bit his bottom lip as he walked her way.

"Take that shit off."

"You take it off."

"Eternity if I take that dress off of you, I'm gonna rip it off."

She smiled at his aggressive ways. She just knew that he was about to split her in ways that she had been dreaming of for months.

"Then rip i—"

He grabbed her sundress at the middle and then pulled roughly in opposite directions, causing the cotton to rip.

"Malikkkkkk."

"You said rip this shit."

He leaned down and covered her neck in kisses. When their lips met, their tongues danced to its own tune. Eternity used her hands to pull down his sweatpants. She ended up pulling down his sweats and his boxers in one movement. Once his dick was out of the material it stood at attention in between his strong thighs. She stopped kissing him to look down at his girth.

That chocolate skin of his drove her crazy. It was the curve and the veins in his member that made her want to taste him, it made her want to feel him. He finished ripping the rest of her dress and then he stepped back to observe her. The bra and thong set she wore was black. He kicked off his sneakers and then stepped completely out of his sweatpants. In front of her he stood with just socks on.

"Take the bra off, leave the thong on."

Eternity did as she was told. She didn't care that her breast hung a little lower since having their son. She knew that Bleek loved her, flaws and all. He loved ever droop, every stretch mark and ever toxic trait of hers.

"Mmm," he hummed once her breast was freed from its confinement.

He loved her body. Those stretch marks across her stomach proved that she had carried life, she had carried a piece of him. He wanted badly for her to do it again. He needed her to.

With all of the drama in the streets he couldn't fathom leaving this world without a piece of him to live on. He walked over to the bed and then spread her legs wider. When he did, she laid back onto the bed.

"Why you so fucking perfect?"

"I'm not…" she looked away from him.

She felt like the furthest thing from it.

"You're perfect for me."

He grabbed her face and then turned it to his. With his other hand he pulled her thong to the side. He kissed her lovingly as he pushed deep into her walls.

"Sssss Malikkkkkk."

She hugged his strength with her garden. He pulled out and then slowly entered her again. His hand cupped her face as she stroked in and out.

"I love youuuu," she cried out.

It was an intimate moment. All of the tricks and rough shit wasn't needed because they were connecting on a different level, on a new level. They had both grown since the last time their bodies became one and as they shared energy a new love was being created.

"Open up for me."

He gathered one of her legs into his forearm to allow himself more access to the deepest part of her. She inched up the bed.

"Don't run, I'm gonna be gentle."

She looked him into his eyes and trusted that he wouldn't hurt her, so she relaxed. This time he pushed a little deeper into her. She wrapped her arms around his back.

"Malik it's too much."

"Na it's not."

He kissed the side of her face.

"Baby it is."

"Na, it's not baby."

"Fuckkkk mmmmmmmm"

"You cumming?"

He could tell by her facial expression that it was on the horizon.

"Yes," she whispered out.

"Don't hold it. Cum..."

"Cum with me."

He smirked. He had been holding his shit since he entered her.

"I'm not pulling out Eternity."

"Okayyy."

Her sex faces mixed with that voice of pleasure had him about to explode. She wrapped her arms around his waist.

"Give me a baby pleaseeeee."

Tears slid down the sides of her face and then pooled into her ears. He kissed them. He didn't give a damn about the salty taste. He grabbed her chin aggressively.

"You sure?"

She shook her head up and down. She grinded her hips in a circular motion that threw him off.

"Fuckkkk," he growled as he filled her up with his essence.

He didn't stop until everything was out and even then, he kept his stroke going until she came again.

When her eyes finished rolling in the back of her head, he kissed her button nose.

"I love you," she said with closed eyes.

"I know."

Her eyes shot open.

"After just dicking me down like that you better say it back."

He chuckled, "I love you."

He pulled out of her and then walked to the bathroom that was attached to the bedroom.

"Bring me a wet rag, pleaseeeee."

"I'm pissing."

"Really Malik? This shit is coming out."

When Bleek came out of the bathroom he saw Eternity with her legs in the air. She was basically on her neck as she tried to keep her legs up so that she did not make a mess on the bed. He laughed hard as hell.

"It's not funnyyyy.... Get a rag out of my suitcase."

"Just run ya ass to the shower I'll bring the towel and rags in there. You look dumb as hell."

She sucked her teeth as he walked out of the room to go to their suitcases. She jumped up from the bed and then ran towards the bathroom.

Boom!

Bleek rushed towards the bathroom with the towels and rags in his hands.

"What the fuck?"

Eternity was sprawled out onto the floor.

"You alright?"

He sat the items in his hand onto the counter and then helped her up.

"Leave me alone because you said run."

She chuckled as she rubbed her elbow when she got up.

"You're so fucking goofy yo."

He kissed the side of her head while she stood in front of him rubbing her knee. He walked past her to turn the shower water on.

"Got me running in here with the soft dick hanging out."

Eternity laughed.

"You should have seen that shit from my view. The shit was swinging as you ran in here."

She laughed as the image replayed in her head.

"Man shut up," he mushed her playfully.

"Let's wash so we can go eat I'm fucking starving."

He opened the glass door for her and then watched as she stepped inside. Her round behind jiggled as he slapped it when she walked past him.

*****

"How you make all this food with no baked Mac and cheese Ma?"

"Well it's rice."

"Riceeee? How you gone cook up collard greens without the macaroni to go with it."

Toya crossed her arms over her chest with an attitude.

"I don't give a fuck about that attitude. I gave you that attitude. Take out what's in the oven. You don't need gloves cause it's not hot."

Toya wobbled over to the oven and then pulled it open.

"You did make it," she squealed when she noticed a small pan of baked macaroni in the oven.

"Yeah, spoiled ass."

"It's the baby I swear."

"Please girl you been spoiled since a little girl and all Ty did was make it worse."

Toya walked over to her mother and then kissed her on the cheek.

"Where the food at cause I smell it."

Toya chuckled. Bleek was always looking for food when he was around.

"We in the kitchen fat ass," she yelled out, "he brought a girl with him this trip," Toya quickly whispered to her mother.

"The same girl that came for my wedding?" Kelsey whispered back.

"Nope it's a new gir— hey y'all."

Toya changed the subject with her mother when Bleek and Eternity walked into the kitchen.

"Hey," Bleek said flatly.

He could tell that he was the topic of discussion upon walking in. It was the look on the two women's faces that gave it away. He quickly got annoyed but then shook the feeling off.

"This is my lady Eternity. Eternity this is Toya's mom, Kelsey but everybody calls her Ke."

Eternity looked at the woman with watery eyes. She knew her, vividly she remembered her. Kelsey stood with a lump in her throat. It had been years since she had seen the girl in front of her.

"It's ummm nice to meet you," Kelsey said with a weak smile.

The hurt expression on Eternity's face could not be masked.

"You too."

"Okay so… were eating outside inside of the tent. Ty should be down soon," Toya said trying to change the mood in the room.

"Umm where's the bathroom?" Eternity asked.

"In that hallway behind you, it's the second door on the left."

"Thanks."

Eternity let go of Bleek's hand and then headed towards the bathroom. Once the door was closed behind her she breathed deeply. There were so many people in and out of her childhood, so she always blocked them out, but she remembered this woman. She was probably one of the only women that her mother kept around that was caring. She was an addict, but she never looked like one. Just looking at her Eternity knew that she had to be clean. There was no way that she wasn't. *What the fuck?* She thought to herself.

"Auntie Ke, Tori won't give me back the doll you gave to me."

Kelsey sat on the dingy couch that was in Machina's living room. She quickly untied the belt from around her arm when she heard Eternity coming her way.

"I said share boo boo. If she's playing with it now wait until she's finished and then you play with it. You're the big sister you have to be kind, okay?"

Kelsey smiled at the little girl sporting box braids in front of her.

"Okay fine."

Eternity walked away from her with a frown on her face. Kelsey sniffed away tears as she thought of her own daughter. She had given her up because she felt like she was too young to have a child. The depression alone sent her on a downward spiral which led her to Machina's door. She never sold her ass to get a fix because she had the looks to get in the pockets of all of the hustlers.

Her biggest secret was that to cope with the guilt of not being a mother to her own child she indulged in drugs. When she found out that Machina had two kids of her own whenever she came over, she brought a toy. One toy to teach the girls to share. As she watched Eternity mope back to her room she thought of her own daughter. They were about the same age.

"If you not gone light that shit up pass it here, I'm feeling sick and you in your head."

"Your daughter came out here that's why."

Kelsey fussed at Machina as she started to fasten the belt back around her arm.

"Girl please okay I been doing this in front of them for years they already know what it is."

Kelsey frowned. She couldn't imagine doing this in front of her child, let alone anyone else. Her own sister didn't even know that she had an addiction. She loosened the belt around her arm and then tossed it and the pack to Machina.

"I'm out."

She knew that the road to recovery was going to be a hard one, but she was determined to get through it. She stayed away from her own child once her addiction had started but she wasn't trying to do it anymore...

Knock, knock

Eternity sniffled away the distant memory and then wiped the lone tear that cascaded down her face.

"I'm coming out," she called out.

"Just open the door please."

Eternity heard a woman's voice. She quickly wiped her face clean. She was grateful that she didn't put on makeup and decided to attend dinner with her natural face.

After looking in the mirror and seeing that her face was free of tears, she pulled the door open. Kelsey stood on the other side with sadden eyes. She walked into the bathroom and then closed the door behind her.

"I'm sorry. My daughter... she just doesn't know that there was ever a drug using side of me."

Eternity tried to brush off the feeling of sadness.

"It's cool."

"No, it's not. I thought about you and your sister so much. You two were literally the reason why I had gotten clean. You girls made me think of my own baby that I had to be clean for."

Eternity's eyes watered because she wished that her mother had that same will power to get clean for her own kids, but she didn't.

She was on her damn death bed because she had chosen the drugs over her own children.

"You was the only person that walked through that door and showed that you gave a shit about me and my sister. So many heartless people spun through that door. The shit that Machina put us, put me through—"

Eternity broke down crying. She quickly wiped at the tears that was rushing down her face. Without permission, Kelsey hugged her. She knew that living in that house had to be hell for those girls.

"But look at the woman you are today. You're standing here gorgeous and you gotta be smart as hell because Bleek doesn't mess with any dummies." Kelsey chuckled as she leaned back and then looked Eternity in the face.

"I'm sorry but look here, God must have put us in the same space again for a reason. There's a reason this is happening."

Eternity slightly smiled.

"You're right."

Knock, Knock

"E you good?"

"Yeah I'm cool. I'll be out in a minute."

She could hear him twisting the knob to the door.

"Umm aight."

When she heard his footsteps get further away from the bathroom door she spoke.

"I won't tell your daughter about your past. You got over that hump and honestly as a child of an addict that never gave that shit up it's embarrassing. If you two relationship is anything like what I had dreamed for me and my mother I wouldn't dare say anything that could possibly change that."

Kelsey sighed in relief.

"Thank you."

She looked down at Eternity's tube dress and saw that it was slightly twisted to the right.

"Fix your dress miss thing."

Eternity looked down and then blushed when she noticed that the seams to her dress wasn't aligned with the sides of her body.

"Thank you," she giggled out.

Before making it back to Ty's house her and Bleek had a good time in the truck for the ride down the road.

"I'll see you out there," Kelsey said with a smile.

"Okay."

𝒞hapter 14

Everyone sat at the table enjoying the food that Kelsey had cooked. Eternity was on her fourth cup of wine and was starting to feel the buzz.

"Yes girl, have another cup because I need me a niece or nephew from this big-headed asshole over here."

"Fuck off fat ass."

Toya picked a piece of her bread roll off and then threw it across the table.

"See I know y'all lost y'all fucking mind. Throwing food across the table like fucking kids," Kelsey fussed.

Tony chuckled while sitting in his seat. He laughed at his wife because of her sassy attitude. He checked the time on his watch.

"Umm, fellas may I speak with you two for a moment."

Both Ty and Bleek looked down the table at Tony. They stood from the table when he did.

"After y'all little talk I'm gone be ready to go."

"Okay my love."

Tony kissed Kelsey lips before walking into the house.

"What's up Tony?"

"Manny wants to meet tonight. He reached out to me about Chiva Blanca. He said that he did not want to reach out to Julian because he felt the slight tension during the last meet when it came to Alessandra."

Bleek was using this time to get away from Chiva Blanca and there it was answers possibly coming his way.

"Meet where?" he asked.

"I own a bistro in the city. I told him that the meeting can happen there."

"Should we be worried about this meeting?" Ty asked.

"No… I have men at the location already and there is no *we*. I told him that I won't be in attendance. He asked that only you go Malik."

"He's not going by his fucking self."

"Bro, I got this," Bleek said to Ty.

He needed answers and if meeting with Manny alone was going to give him those then he was going.

"I don't know how to feel about this."

"I wouldn't allow him to walk into anything that I felt was a trap."

Ty looked Tony's way and then shook his head up and down. He knew that Tony wouldn't bring any harm their way but not being by his brother's side did not sit well with him.

"What time is the meeting?" Bleek asked.

"Now…"

"What?"

Tony snickered at Bleek's facial expression before putting his hands in his pockets.

"He's on our territory. He can wait a little. Go tell your lady that you will see her later."

Tony headed back outside towards the backyard. Bleek followed behind him. When he made it outside, he saw that Toya was slowly falling asleep in her chair.

"Get ya wife bro for her heavy ass head make her lean over and fall out the chair."

"Fuck off ugly."

Bleek chuckled. They had that rough relationship that was all love.

"Come on ma."

He held his hand out for Eternity.

"We're leaving already?"

"Yes, I need to make a run really quick. I want to make sure that you get in the house safely before I do so."

"A run?" she asked with a raised eyebrow.

"We'll talk in the car. See y'all at breakfast," Bleek said as he walked with Eternity towards the door to exit.

During the ride down the road Bleek had explained everything to Eternity.

"I don't know how I feel about you going by yourself."

"Ma, I'm good."

Eternity sighed. She had a bad feeling about it, but she knew that he was going to go regardless. The only thing that she could do was pray for his safety. Bleek unlocked the front door for her.

"You gone wait up for me?" he asked with a smirk.

"Hell fucking no, as tired as I am," she said in a bratty tone as she rolled her eyes.

"Give me kiss."

She looked at him with those chocolate lips puckered out and then she shyly smiled. She smashed her lips against his. He bit her bottom lip gently and then sucked on it before ending their kiss.

"Wait up for me, ma."

"Okay."

He nodded his head towards the house.

"Go ahead, go."

She started to walk away and then looked back at him. He closed the front door and then locked it before walking back to the truck to make his way to Tony's bistro in the city.

***

"This is it sir."

Bleek looked out the window at the small bistro that was located on the corner. It was a quaint space that stuck out among the other small businesses that surrounded it.

"Stay parked here. I shouldn't be long."

The driver nodded his head and then opened his door so that he could walk around to open the door for Bleek.

"I got it."

Bleek opened his own door and then made his way to the establishment. When he walked inside, he saw that the space was empty except for one booth in the back that was occupied. He noticed Manny sitting in it with a glass of cognac sitting in front of him on the table. He swaggered over to the table and then sat into the booth next to him.

"I thought you weren't going to come meng."

"Had other shit to take care of. So, what's up?"

Manny took a sip of his drink and then placed it back onto the table before speaking.

"My niece is out of control you know. I heard about that shooting in South Beach. That isn't how we do things."

"You can't really say how *we* do things when you ain't running shit anymore."

"Oh, but I can because I still very much run my cartel. She is just improvising, and I don't like it."

"Okay that makes two of us."

"You know Chiva was always the most aggressive of all my nieces. Her father, my youngest brother, before he died was just like that. A loose cannon. It was something I always despised, that's why I killed him."

Bleek's eyes opened massively.

"I killed my own brother for the same exact shit that I am letting his daughter do freely. Chiva finally told me about this bone she has with you."

"Oh yeah? What's that?"

"My niece had a sister. Her mother had given birth to another girl four years after she was born. After I killed my brother, I gave his wife the option of sending that daughter to the states for a better living, but I told her that I would raise Chiva because she was my blood through my brother. Her sister had a father that was a milk runner in the town. The poor bastard could barely fend for himself let alone a fucking child."

Bleek sat back into the cushioned chair as he listened.

"Chiva says that you are responsible for the death of her sister."

Bleek screwed his face. Now he knew damn well that her beef with him was unnecessary.

"She got the wrong guy. My list is long, but I've never killed a woman."

Manny opened his suit jacket and when he did Bleek instantly regretted not taking a gun from Ty's house. He pulled out a piece of loose-leaf paper and then placed it onto the table.

"But it seems as if you have. Chiva has been having the groundskeepers at her sister's resting place gather everything left at the grave since she was buried. Last year this note here ended up there. I guess someone that visited left it there or had it sent there."

Manny yawned and then stretched in his chair.

"This is way past my sleep time. Keep the note. I will say this to you meng, my niece isn't going to stop until you're dead. Now that, I can assist you with."

When Manny rose from his seat, Bleek spoke.

"Assist me with fucking what? Being dead? I'll pass."

Manny chuckled.

"She just needs to believe it meng."

Bleek heard him but he really wasn't listening.

"Man, you already offed one of your family members for the same shit that she is doing why not just get rid of her for old times' sake."

"It's not that easy. Doing something like that weighs on the soul heavy. There is no way I will do it again but what I will do is let you know when you can. Goodnight Malik." Bleek shook his head.

"Yeah aight man, goodnight."

He knew that Mexican cartels was ruthless, but he didn't know to this extent. The man walking out of the bistro had killed his own brother and had offered up his assistance to kill his niece, the girl he had raised. He couldn't picture himself putting a bullet in Ty and he wasn't even his blood. He blew out a sharp breath and then opened the folded paper that rested on the table in front of him.

I don't even know where to start Leah...
I can't stop the tears from falling with this one. Now like I always do for the holidays, your birthday etc. I write you a letter to get shit off my chest. As soon as I send it off, I swear I feel ten times better, but something tells me that after this one, I'm not gonna feel better at all.

I'm thinking about leaving him. I know… I know you probably shaking ya head doubting me, but this shit is unforgivable to me. I don't think there is an us getting past this and you know we had a lot of shit to get past over the years. For years Leah, I have been thinking about your death. A drive-by shooting? We bad bitches sis, that's not how one of us was supposed to go.

Those damn Brooklyn drive-by cases go on for years without a lick of a suspect. I can't sleep at night because I know who was responsible for yours. The man I love was the one that put the hit out for that night, and I know that it wasn't for you specifically but still I can't stop myself from feeling this way. How can I look the man I call brother in the face knowing that he was responsible for your death?

You shared a bed with him, and he did this to you. What bothers me most is that I don't think that it even bothers him. This game has turned him and Ty into fucking monsters. They commit the unthinkable and then they are able to sleep at night. I feel like I can't do this shit Leah… I can't breathe knowing that Malik is responsible for killing you. Pray for me girl, God knows that I pray for your soul every single day. I love you…
Toya

Bleek's breathing started to pick up. Because of this exact shooting he changed the entire way he moved in the streets. He felt a hallow feeling in the pit of his stomach because not only was he shocked that Toya knew but she had written it down on paper. This note could have him under the jail if placed in the wrong hands. This was the same exact shooting that had him wanted in the state of New York a few years back before the case was dismissed.

"Is she really this fucking stupid?" he mumbled to himself.

He knew that Ty had to be the one to tell her because when it had first happened, he was the one that told him. He knew that his brother kept Toya in the loop with certain things, but it was never street shit. Growing up, she was just that girl that wanted to be around the hood niggas. She didn't have a hood bone in her body. Eternity on the other hand, she was as hood, as they came. That is why anything that occurred outside in that jungle that he called the streets he disclosed with her. She had that hustlers mentality and that gangsta mindset that kept him grounded.

He folded the paper and then leaned up in his seat to put it into his pocket. He was fuming. He had one of his trucks robbed with one of his drivers killed, his house trashed, his safety was on the line and he was shot at all because Toya had to *get some shit* off her chest. *We could have hired a private therapist for all of this shit,* he thought to himself as he sucked his teeth. After trying to compose himself, he finally stood from the booth to make his way back to the house.

***

"Hey you."

Eternity woke when she heard Bleek turn his key into the front door. She cleared her throat and then rolled over in the bed to face the door. He didn't say anything in return as he came out of his clothes.

"What's wrong boo?"

After undoing his belt and then pulling his jeans to his ankles, he stepped out of them.

"Malik?"

"Ma… just let me hold you and I'll put you on in the morning. Please…"

She could sense the frustration in his tone. He was off and she felt the vibe as soon as he was close enough to her. He got into the bed and when he did, she scooted backward so that her back was up against his chest. He threw his arm over her and then pulled her close. He was blessed to have someone as thorough as her.

She had put him through so much pain over the past years but when it came to street shit, she was solid. She knew how to play the role. She would right hand on the bible lie for a nigga and he had to appreciate that.

"I love you," she whispered.

He kissed the nape of her neck and then sniffed in her scent. That vanilla fragrance always got to him.

Eternity closed her eyes and then listened to the natural sounds of the land. The sound of water hitting the oceans rock was soothing. Bleek on the other hand couldn't sleep. His mind was bothered. When he looked at the clock on the nightstand, he saw that it was three in the morning. He lifted his head up to see if Eternity was sleeping. Her light snore confirmed her sleeping state to him. He carefully slipped out of bed. When he went to the closet, he saw that Eternity had unpacked their things in his absence.

C. Wilson

He took a pair of sweatpants off of the shelf and a shirt. He looked on the carpeted floor and saw that a pair of his slides were there. He slipped his feet into the slippers and then walked back into the room. He dug into the pockets of his jeans, got the folded paper out and then put it in the pocket of his sweatpants. After grabbing the keys off of the nightstand, he headed out. There was a club car waiting out front and he prayed that one of the keys on the ring to the house keys was for the car. He sat in the driver's seat and tried every key until he got the right one.

When the car started, he backed out of the driveway and then headed towards Ty's house. He was driving so fast that wind started to gather into his shirt which caused it to flap with the breeze. He pulled up to Ty's house and then cut the engine to the club car. He used his key to get in. When he walked into the kitchen Ty's back was facing him. He was standing at the counter making himself a sandwich. Ty turned around quickly with a gun in his hand.

"Shit bro damn," he said once he realized that only Bleek was behind him.

"All those fucking guards you got outside, and you still worried about somebody running in this shit."

"I will never not worry. It's guns hidden all around this muthafucka."

Ty put the gun he just had in his hand back into drawer that was slightly open next to him.

"What you doing down here? You hungry?"

"Na, I'm not hungry."

"How did the meeting go?"

Ty sat down on one of the stools that sat in front of the kitchen island.

Bleek stood on the other side of the marble countered island. He rested his forearms onto the surface.

"Got more information than I expected."

Ty took a bite of his sandwich. With a mouthful he spoke.

"Fill me in, what's up."

Bleek moved his head around in a circular motion to give some relief to his neck. He wanted to rid his body of the tension he felt period. He reached into the pocket of his sweatpants and then tossed the folded paper onto the top of the countertop.

"Fuck is this?"

Ty put his sandwich down onto his plate.

"Just read it."

Bleek watched as Ty picked up a nearby napkin to wipe his hands clean and then he slid the paper in his direction. After opening the note, he began to read it. Bleek could see his brother's bushy eyebrows scrunch into anger as his eyes quickly skimmed over the paper.

"Ain't no way Toya wrote this shit."

Ty was in denial. He knew that the handwriting belonged to his wife.

"What the fuck was she thinking? What the fuck was she eve—"

"How does she even know?"

Ty looked up at Bleek and then sighed. He knew that he had fucked up when he had come clean about it.

Even with him coming clean to his wife the year prior what he should have done was keep his brother out of it.

"Bro we was going through a rough patch and—"

"Ima keep it a hundred with you right now. This is my fucking life! You hit a rough patch with your bitch, and you start yapping about my fucking criminal activity."

"Watch ya mouth."

Ty stood from his stool. He understood why Bleek was upset but calling his wife a bitch in front of him wasn't going to fly.

"I ain't watching shit and you might as well sit the fuck back down. We both know I'll break ya ass up in this kitchen. You ain't been solid ever since you got shot. This Chiva Blanca bitch wants my fucking head because of your wife!"

Bleek didn't mean to yell but all of his emotions was bottled up. He was fed the fuck up. His comment about Ty getting shot was a low blow and he knew it, but in the moment, he didn't give a fuck. He started to understand why Manny could kill his flesh and blood. It was a kill or be killed world out there.

"Bleek... you pissed I know."

"I'm fucking beyond it. I ain't ever bring no shit like this to you. You ain't ever have to walk the streets with your head on a swivel because of me. I'm the nigga that get you out of shit. I'm fucking solid. This bitch shot at me and *my* family. You here protected in a fortress with yours. What the fuck about mine?"

He beat on his own chest with his last words.

"Bro, I'm sorry."

It was the only thing that Ty could say. Bleek was talking facts so Ty didn't have a counter. Reading the part in the letter where Toya said that she was going to leave him didn't even sting because he knew that. He felt it a year ago, he felt them falling apart. That's why he made it his business to try and wine and dine her and just when he thought that things were done, he knocked her up. It was selfish but he was willing to do anything to keep his family together.

Bleek and Ty stared at one another. Two men born of different wombs but built from the same cloth. Ty didn't think when trying to save his marriage just how he had put his brother at a disadvantage. He mistaken the sturdiness of his lady when it came to the street shit.

"I'm sorry," Ty said again.

"Yeah, I bet."

Bleek turned to walk out of the kitchen and Ty let him. He knew that he had to give his brother his space.

He would handle Toya later on the fuck up that she had did. He understood her writing letters to her dead best friend, it was a coping mechanism, but he never knew of her physically sending them off anywhere. When he heard his front door slam, he sighed. Shortly after, he heard his youngest daughter crying out of her sleep from the disturbance. He stood from the stool and then rotated his arm in a circular motion. Bleek was right about him not being one hundred after the shooting. He shook his head again because he didn't know what he could do to get back in his brother's good graces.

***

"Wake up," Bleek shook Eternity out of her sleep.

"Mmmm," she grumbled as she turned over in the sheets.

"Ma wake that ass up. We out."

Eternity blinked her eyes repeatedly until she was able to open them completely without the light in the room burning her pupils.

"Where are we going?" she asked in a groggy tone.

"We're going back to Miami."

"But we just got here," she whined.

"And now we're just leaving."

She sat up in the bed and saw that Bleek had their suitcases open out on the floor with their clothes inside.

"Baby what's wrong?" she asked as she watched him walk in and out of the closet.

"I promise I'm gonna tell you on the jet, right now I just need you to put this on," he threw a pair of sweatpants, a shirt, and a pair of socks onto the bed, "get dressed and lets go."

She stood up from the bed, stretched and then walked over to the bathroom. After emptying her bladder, she grabbed the clothes off of the bed and then started to dress in them. It took them no time to pack the rest of their belongings and then get in the truck that was going to take them to the airstrip. As they settled in on the jet, Bleek filled her in with everything.

"Honestly, boo, you know I'm gone always keep it tall with you, she was mourning and trying to get through it. You can't really be mad at her for that."

"I'm not mad at her at all she's a female and females are emotional."

His tone was dead and lacked the sympathy that she had.

Eternity raised her eyebrow and then crossed her arms over her chest.

"No, the fuck we are not. Well not all of us."

"You know what I mean Ma. The point is I'm not mad at her, I'm mad at my brother for this shit."

"Well you can't even get mad at him for that either. You can't fault him for assuming that he had a solid chick at his side. My sister would have never done some shit like that," she mumbled the last part under her breath. Bleek knew that she was right but that still didn't stop him from being upset.

*C*hapter 15

One month later...

Eternity rushed around the room as she tossed clothes into her carry-on bag. In a month's time the youth center would be done with the construction on the site. She wanted to be as hand's on as possible.

"Malik..." she called out.

Bleek strolled into the room eating an apple. Instead of responding to her he just stood in the doorway.

"You didn't pack shit yet. We need to be in New York by the morning."

"I told you whatever needed to be signed we could do it electronically."

She stopped packing her bag and then folded her arms as she looked at him.

"And I told you that I wanted to see what was done already. You've been paying construction workers and interior decorators. You don't want to see what they have completed?"

"They sent pictures Eternity."

"That's not good enough for me. I need to physically be in the space to see if I like it."

They stared at each other. When she poked her bottom lip out, he caved.

"Well there's no need to pack anything. We are going and coming right the fuck back. I already told you that I don't feel comfortable being out of Florida anymore." Eternity knew that Bleek was still on guard when it came to the woman named Chiva Blanca.

"Fine."

She zipped the duffle bag she was just packing closed and then tossed it onto the floor near the bed.

"Well go on, make whatever calls you need to so that we can get there and get back."

He smirked at her spoiled ways. He walked out of the room to go call his pilot for a last-minute flight.

***

"You sitting over there creasing your damn forehead up what are you stressing about? You saw the space and said you loved it and going forward if something is being done that you don't like then we can put a stop to it."

Eternity listened as she watched Bleek buckle the seat belt across his lap. She did the same before she responded.

"I know, it's just my first business you know. I just want it to be perfect."

She had this funny feeling in the pit of her stomach. She knew that it had to be the random sickness she would get throughout the day. She knew that she was pregnant she just didn't want to take a test to confirm it.

To her, it was already a blessing that her and Bleek was getting a second chance at love. She just knew that there was no way that she could catch a blessing twice. She feared carrying a child because she just knew that some way, somehow, she would have the opportunity of being a mother again snatched from her.

She rubbed her stomach to soothe some of the nausea that she knew would intensify as soon as the jet started to rise from the airstrip.

"You good?" Bleek asked with a raised eyebrow. Eternity shook her head up and down as she lightly rubbed her stomach. He leaned over and placed his big hand over hers.

"You know telling me isn't going to jinx anything right?"

She looked him in his eyes with this confused look on her face.

"How did you—"

"Eternity besides me knowing your body like I know my own, those green wrappers you leave in the bathroom garbage during your monthly wasn't there last month. That shit was a dead giveaway."

She felt like she could breathe a little. She knew her body and the moment she missed the first day of her period she already knew that she was pregnant. She hadn't been on birth control and Bleek wasn't pulling out. This wasn't something that they was trying to prevent but it wasn't something that they were planning either.

"I'm scared," she admitted.

"I am too but this time we're together for the shit."

"Okay Mr. Browne it looks like the storm is heading the other way back down towards the gulf coast, so we are clear to take off." The pilot said as he peeked his head out of the cockpit.

"Okay thank you."

Bleek felt his phone vibrating in his pocket. When he saw that it was Ty FaceTime calling him, he ignored the call and then put his phone on airplane mode. The two still had not spoken since Bleek had left that early morning after their dispute. A stewardess came out of the cockpit and then sat in a singular chair near the exit door.

"As soon as we are in the air you two can tell me if you want anything to drink or to snack on and I will get it okay?" She said as she fasten her seat belt.

In no time the jet started to move down the airstrip. Eternity closed her eyes tightly and then breathed deeply.

"You been flying back and forth for too long to still be acting like this."

Bleek kissed her button nose and then grabbed her hand before resting his head back on his seat. Flying had become second nature to him. As the jet soared through the clouds, they finished their conversation.

"I wouldn't even know what to name him if it's a boy."

"It's not even about to be a boy. It's gonna be a girl because her big brother won't have it any other way."

Bleek rubbed her flat stomach and then smiled.

"Is there anything that I can get for you both? Juice? Snacks?"

"An apple juice," Eternity said with a smile.

"Give me a water and some cookies."

"Okay mam I have that and Mr. Browne just the water and cookies?"

"Yup"

"Okay I'll be right back."

The flight attendant went to an area in the rear of the jet to prepare their request. Bleek pulled down the tables in front of him and Eternity so that their drinks could sit.

"We need a pretty girl name."

"Yeah, something unique but nothing too crazy that's hard to pronounce."

Eternity smiled. This is the shit she was missing her first pregnancy. Although Vincent was there the whole time, they didn't share moments like this. This felt right, these were moments she was supposed to share with the love of her life the first time around.

"Here you go."

The stewardess placed two cups of ice down onto the table. She opened a bottle water and then poured it into one cup and then opened a canned apple juice and then poured it into the other. After handing Bleek a pack of cookies she started to push the tray towards the back.

"Is the plane tilting?"

"What?" Bleek asked.

Eternity looked at her cup and noticed how the apple juice was settling towards the left side of the cup.

"Is this fucking plane tilting!?" She started to panic.

"Ma calm down he's probably making a turn."

The stewardess walked quickly from the rear of the jet towards the front.

"Captain?" She called out as she knocked on the door of the cockpit.

She turned the handle, but the door was locked.

"Captain?" She called again as she knocked a little harder this time.

In an instant the plane started to drop causing her to fall to the floor. She hit her head on the knob on the way down and now laid unconscious in front of Bleek and Eternity.

"What the fuck?" Bleek said as placed one arm over the front of Eternity to shield her.

Tears streamed down her face faster than the jet descending.

"I don't want to die!"

She was finally starting to feel like she was living and look. She felt like during her whole life, happiness never stayed. It was always a temporary thing, something that just wasn't meant for her.

"Eternity look at me. Focus on me Ma."

She opened her eyes and looked into his.

His stare was calm. They were in a jet that was crashing, and his masculine face was calming her.

"Do you trust me?" he asked.

She shook her head up and down as she sniffed tears away.

"I need you to say it."

"I trust you."

"Do you love me?" He asked.

"I love you."

"We gone be good."

The lights in the aircraft went out and when they did Bleek leaned over and kissed Eternity. Both of their stomachs went hallow. It was the feeling you get on a rollercoaster just only ten times worse. After their kiss he tapped her lips gently.

"We gone be good."

He said again in more of a whisper....

𝒞hapter 16

"Tori you need to get out of bed...."

She heard him standing in the doorway, but his statement went on deaf ears. Nobody could tell her how to feel. She had lost two of the closest people to her. She knew that he was hurting too but to her, no one's hurt could compare to hers. *How the fuck does a plane crash with no bodies found?* She wondered as she soaked her feathered pillow in tears.

"Tori..."

"Just get the fuck out," she mumbled.

She wasn't ready to get out of bed she didn't give a damn that it had been a year since Bleek, and Eternity had been gone. The pain felt like it happened just yesterday. Deep down she regretted treating Sha the way she was but on the other hand she didn't give a fuck.

He was working hard running mechanical shops, her beauty bar and all of his other investments but still, she couldn't shake the mood she had been in. She wondered why God had to take so many people she loved from her. Within five years she had lost a nephew, her own child, a love she thought was so pure and then her sister and brother. *Why?* She used her hand to ball some of the sheets up as she cried harder. She felt weight being applied onto the other part of the bed that was behind her.

"We gotta do better."

Sha had so much patience with her. He too was hurting but he put his grieving on the back burner to console her.

"Just leave me... alone."

She was barely audible because the tears had her choked up.

"No."

He kicked off his sneakers and then laid down in the bed behind her. He spooned her and then moved her messy hair out of her face.

"Baby girl you loss so much weight. We have to do better."

He kissed the side of her head and then gently he rocked back and forth as he held her in his strong arms. She started to drift off into sleep. He knew exactly what to do and what to say to ease her mind even if it was only temporarily just to get her to sleep for the night. Once he heard her lightly snoring, he got up from the bed. He had been draining himself for a year keeping a secret. He prayed that soon enough he could breathe again but he knew that wouldn't happen until he was able to come clean.

His ringing phone made him walk quickly around the bed and to the nightstand to answer it before the noise could wake Tori. When the number started with "011" Sha knew exactly who was calling him. He answered the phone without saying a word.

"It's time."

He heard in his ear and then the line went dead. Sha changed out of the clothes he was wearing and into all black. It was indeed time, time to put in work.

***

He entered the lavish living room and then smiled when he saw her silhouette on the other side of the silk curtains that covered the full windows to the balcony. He pulled back the sheer white drapes and then watched as she rocked his baby girl in her arms.

"Is she finally asleep?" Bleek asked.

"She is."

Eternity's smile was bright. He loved to see a smile plastered on her face. That was her permanent facial expression ever since she had given birth to their daughter. This was the happiness he had been promising her for years. He held onto the brass banister of the balcony and overlooked the Paris skyline. The lights reminded him of New York, which made him think of Miami.

"Malik, when can we go back home?"

It was like she was reading his mind or something.

"This Chiva Blanca bitch wants to take everything from me. The moment I suspected you being pregnant I knew I had to do what would be best for us. We can't go back home until I have her in the ground. Don't worry Ma, I got somebody working on it."

"Somebody like who? Who else knows that we're alive?"

"Don't even worry about it. You trust me?"

"I trust you." She said without hesitation.

"Do you love me?"

"I love you."

He kissed her forehead and then slapped her lightly on her butt. It jiggled in the silk robe she wore.

"Go put her down in the crib. I know you healed up it's time to work on baby number two."

He smirked as she walked into the condo. When she was inside, he pulled out a burner cellphone from his pocket, dialed a number and then waited for it to ring.

When the ringing stopped in his ear, he knew that the person had answered.

"It's time." Bleek simply said before ending the line. He stood on the balcony for a while until Eternity's voice interrupted his thoughts.

"I put her in her crib and she's still sleeping." She had a sexy tone in her voice that caused him to turn around. When he saw that she was as naked as the day she was born instantly he became brick hard.

"Get out here."

She tip toed off of the carpet of the inside and onto the tile of the balcony.

"I fucking love you." He admitted.

He turned her around and dropped his basketball shorts and boxer briefs in one swift move.

"I love youuuuu…" she cooed as he parted her from behind.

They had a lot of drama ahead of them but at least they were finally together. They were finally getting that *hood* happily ever after.

THE END?

A note from C. Wilson

Y'all know I play too much. Flip the page to finish reading

Sha sat parked in a rental car with paper tags. In his lap he held his 9mm pistol. He looked at the Mexican bar a few buildings up from him. Bleek had told him what time he should arrive, and he was ten minutes early. He pressed a button on the magazine of his gun to make sure that he had a full clip. He sat in silence. No radio and no one accompanied him for this drill. Bleek was usually the one at his side when it was time to put in work. He watched as Manny walked towards the bar. He still couldn't believe that the man that just walked in front of his vehicle set this whole thing up.

He was the one that told Bleek that his own niece wouldn't stop coming for him unless he was dead. He staged Bleek's death and now it was him setting up his own flesh and blood. Bleek was assured that the guards all knew that the night was the night for Chiva Blanca to die. Sha looked at the clock on his car. It was time. He cut his engine, quickly twisted a silencer nub onto the nose of his pistol and then exited the car. He stood crouched down in between two SUV's.

The block was silent. Not even the Miami party goers were out. Sha felt his heart beating out of his chest. It didn't matter how many runs he had like this, it always felt like the first time to him. He heard a pair of heels hitting the pavement.

"Chivaaa… hello my love."

"Hola Tio."

Sha peeked from behind the truck and saw that Manny and his niece was embracing in a hug. The woman's back was facing him, but he had to admire her physique briefly. Her long brown hair fell down her back in curls. She wore a fitted red sweater dress with some cheetah pumps on her feet.

When Sha and Manny made eye contact, Sha took his shot. The bullet glided through the air silently and struck her in the back.

"Ahhhh Tio, someone is shooting!"

She fell into her uncle only for him to catch her in his arms. Chiva looked around at her guards and saw that no one was retaliating. Then is when Sha knew that he had the green light. He walked towards the bar.

"That is enough! I will take her inside to die."

Manny looked at Sha with pleading eyes.

"To die? Tio what is going on?" Chiva asked in a whisper.

She felt the bullet moving around in her body. When she tasted blood in her mouth, she knew that if she didn't get taken to a hospital and quickly that she would die.

"I don't leave food on my plate," Sha said as he continued towards the bar.

As bad as Manny wanted to fight Sha on his decision to finish the job right there, he couldn't. If the shoe were on the other foot, he would need to see someone like Chiva die. She was reckless, careless, and risky all under his name.

"Tio, what is this?"

"You are reckless my love just like your father was. I'm sorry its nothing that I will tolerate."

"But he killed my sister," she cried out.

"And your sister was not one of us. She was not my blood. That alone makes the situation none of mine."

Manny didn't care that his niece was tainting his cream-colored sweater crimson, he wouldn't let go of her until her last breath was taken. When Sha made it to the steps of the bar, he still had his gun in hand. He wanted to get a head shot and go about his business but the pain in the woman eyes as she was slowly dying halted him.

"Have your men take her inside, she doesn't have much more time."

Manny looked at Sha and then shook his head quickly.

"Thank you," was all that he said before ordering his men to bring his niece inside of his business for her to take her final breaths.

Once the door to the establishment was closed Sha took a deep breath. He pulled a burner cellphone from his pocket and then placed a call. When the phone stopped ringing because someone answered he spoke.

"It's done. Bring y'all asses home asap because I'm explaining everything to Tori tomorrow. For a fucking year she have not been right."

Sha heard sigh in his ear.

***

Bleek sighed before he spoke.

"We will be there in the morning."

"Yeah aight, come to my crib that's where we will be."

Sha hung up before Bleek could respond. Bleek sat on the couch in his new home with the phone still in his hand. He knew that Sha was still angry at him for leaving everything on his shoulders. It wasn't fair and he knew it, but he had to do what was in the best interest for all of them.

His own brother didn't even know that he was still alive. For a year he let Ty, Toya and Tori mourn him.

"What's wrong?"

"We're going home tomorrow."

Eternity looked at Bleek as if she had heard him incorrectly.

"Is it safe?"

"Ma we are going home."

His voice cracked as his chest heaved up and down. For the past year he had been beating himself up thinking that his way of going about things were the wrong way. Tears fell down his face as he chest shook.

"We are going home."

She crossed the room and then sat into his lap. With her hands she wiped his face.

She wrapped her arms around him and then kissed all over his face. He was letting all of these emotions out that he had been holding in for an entire year. She had never known that this is how he was feeling. If she did, she would have dialed back a bit on nagging about them going home.

"Shhh, shhh," she told him as she wiped his face again.

"When it comes to this street shit, I'm a fucking failure ma. I let a bitch… a fucking woman run me off. My own fucking brother think we dead. I couldn't even tell him because I needed the shit to be so real. This bitch had eyes everywhere. I needed her to believe that we were gone."

"I know, you did what you had to. Listen, they gone be mad but with time they will understand. You good?"

She looked him in the eyes. He had been consoling and saving her for as long as he could remember that it felt amazing having her be the one to put him together.

"I'm straight."

She kissed his lips.

"Good because it's time to start packing."

The smile she wore was golden. He hadn't seen her smile like *that* since she had pushed their daughter out. Over the year she expressed moments of happiness but the smile he had just seen was one she wore during her happiest moments. He watched her walk away and when she was out of his sights he leaned back into the couch. After throwing his head, he blew out a sharp breath.

"We going home…"

$\mathcal{C}$hapter 17

Sha was grateful that the night before Tori was sleep when he came in. He had eased out of the bed early to make her some breakfast. Today was the day. He was finally going to come clean about what he had been hiding for a year. The two people in the world that was capable of keeping the secret of knowing that Bleek and Eternity were still alive couldn't know because they were also the same people that would make their death look so real. Their mourning was the icing on the cake for Chiva Blanca. It's what made her lower her guard.

He aggressively scraped the eggs in the frying pan that was starting to stick. Breakfast wasn't his forte, but he was trying.

"You know damn well that you can't cook."
Sha laughed because he could see that Tori was in a good mood this morning which was rare.

"Man shut up you still gone eat the shit."

"Yeah cause ain't shit else to eat in here, might as well."

He turned around and saw that she was sitting on the counter behind him.

"What I tell you about sitting ya ass on the countertops?"

"Please, okay. You don't say shit when you fucking me up here so leave me alone."

She took a banana out of the fruit bowl behind her and then began to peel it.

"Here take a bite," she said with a smile while she held the banana his way.

He screwed his face up. She just knew that some smart shit was going to come out of his mouth.

"You better break a piece off and then give it to me. I'm not about to bite on a damn banana fuck I look like. I'll break that shit up into pieces, shake them in my hand like sunflower seeds and then eat them before I take a bite of a whole banana."

She burst into laughter. Moments like this didn't come around often within the last year but it was something about the day.

Tori woke up with a different mindset. She was at the point in her life where she wanted to let go. For the past year she knew that she had been a lot to deal with and she was blessed to have Sha in her corner. He was patient and considering that he was hurting too his way of dealing with her made her fall in love with him.

"Thank you."

"For what the laugh? Shitttt I'm dead ass."

"Not for that," she giggled, "for holding it down this past year. You have been mourning just like me and you continuously make it your business to put me first. I know I've been a handful, but you still work with me."

Sha felt like shit. He looked away from her and then turned around to fix her plate.

"Babe, did you hear me?"

Ding, dong

"Expecting somebody?"

Sha turned around to find Tori with her arms crossed over her breast and with a raised eyebrow. No one knew where he lived and for a year besides a delivery for her, no one ever rang the bell.

"I really hope you don't hate me after this shit."

Tori looked at him with a confused facial expression.

"Hate you for what?"

She jumped down from the countertop and then followed him to the door.

"For this."

Sha pulled the front door open and when Tori's eyes landed on Bleek and her sister she held onto the stair's banister behind her for support. She felt sick to her stomach.

"Hi Tori Tee."

Tears filled Eternity's eyes as she looked at younger sister. She had lost a lot of weight but that didn't take from her beauty. She stepped into the doorway of the house only for Tori to take a step backward. Sha backed up to give the two sisters their space. His eyes glanced at Bleek and then gave him a quick head nod.

"Tori…"

Eternity knew that she had to be careful with her words and with her movements but when she saw what looked like her sister hyperventilating, she rushed to her side.

"Put your arms up and breathe slowly."

Snot and tears poured down Tori's face.

"Get the fuck away from me!"

The scene was heartbreaking.

"Get the fuck away from me," she cried out again.

"No, I'm here."

Eternity hugged her sister.

"I thought you were dead. I thought you both were fucking dead."

Tori looked at the door and made eye contact with Bleek.

"How could y'all do this to me?"

She pushed Eternity away from her. As quickly as the pain of sadness overwhelmed her anger replaced it. Tori cut her eyes at Sha.

"You fucking knew?"

"Tori…" Bleek called out to her.

He could already see all of the rage built up in her and she was about to unleash it on the man that had been there for her for the past year.

"You fucking knew, huh?"

Before anybody could do anything, Tori threw a punch that landed on the side of Sha's head. He threw his arms up and used his forearms as a shield against her blows.

"Tori!" Bleek stood in between them only to catch two punches to his head.

She quickly turned around and faced her sister.

"I've been living in hell for the past year."

"Tori Tee I know. I swear it was for the best we would have never—"

Slap!

Eternity quickly raised her hand to her face. The sting of the blow made the whole side of face feel hot.

"Oh, we get punched in the fucking face and you only slap her. Punch her ass too," Sha's tone was sarcastic. He stood behind Tori still rubbing the side of his head from the blow that she delivered.

"You know what, you're right."
She lifted her arm with the balled fist at the end to attack her sister but Bleek tossed his arms around her and then lifted her off her feet. He had her hands pinned at her sides.

"Let me the fuck go!"

"No."

He walked to the living room with her in his arms. She kicked wildly but that didn't loosen the grip that he had on her. When he made it in front of the couch, he let go of her and then tossed her onto the chair. She went to jump back up, but he pushed her back down.

"This shit was my decision you not about to sit here and be mad at nobody else BUT me."
Tori looked away from him and focused her sights on Eternity and Sha that was just now entering the room.

"I was stressed the fuck out. My hair fell out, my weight left me. I was sitting here fucking mourning nothing. Look at y'all your beard is all full and she's fat as fuck I guess y'all was living great, huh?"

Bleek shook his head because he knew that when Tori was upset that the inner brat in her came out. He knew that Eternity had been insecure about the extra pounds she had put on after the birth of their daughter. When he looked back at her he could tell that her feelings was hurt. She sucked it up though because no one in the room could imagine what Tori had felt for the past year.

"We had a daughter."

Tori looked up at Bleek and then her eyes softened.

"Where is she?"

"Back home with the nanny. I didn't want to bring her out here until you two were given a chance to speak and get past this."

Tori looked at Eternity and then rolled her eyes.

"Sorry about the fat comment I'm sure it's just baby weight."

She said with sass as she folded one leg over the other.

"Well shit can I get a sorry for you punching me in the fucking head?" Sha asked.

Everyone in the room laughed.

"Y'all laughing shitttt I'm dead ass."

Tori looked her sister in the eyes.

"Who else knew?"

Eternity looked to Bleek because she didn't know who knew she just knew who didn't.

"Only Sha."

"Ty doesn't know?" Tori asked with disbelief.

"No, he doesn't know."

Tori shook her head. She wanted to still be angry, but she felt relief. Her sister and her brother were standing in front of her. She felt the weight of what felt like cement be lifted from her chest. It was exhausting carrying that load around for a year.

"Where do we go from here?"

Tori was talking to Eternity. Her body was still shaking from seeing her sister standing in front of her.

"I want you to come to Paris to meet your niece."

"Paris!? Oh, y'all was really living it the fuck up. Bitch let me go get my beret and my striped shirt. We can go like right now. Can y'all say oui oui?"

Everyone in the room started laughing when Tori stood from the couch and put one of her fingers up like she had class.

"Are we making this a family trip?" Eternity looked to Bleek and asked.

"I need to go to D.R to see my brother."

"You better make your presence known before you go all the way out there. That nigga Ty been on some crazy shit since you been gone. I'm talking he tripled his security at the crib and he just been moving funny Tony said."

Sha had to let Bleek know that a pop up visit would most likely be unwanted. Ty didn't get much visitors these days. Bleek listened but he knew that a phone call wouldn't do it. He needed to see his brother in person.

"Ima just go out there."

"You want me to go with you?" Sha asked.

"Na, you can go to Paris with the girls."

"Shit… you ain't got to tell me twice I've never been."

***

C. Wilson

Traveling to the Dominican Republic without the
luxury of his jet was annoying. Manny had gotten both he
and Eternity new identification when they faked their deaths.
He walked around outside of the airport until he hit the taxi
center. He had to dig in the back of his mind to even get the
address. He was so used to just hopping in a tinted Escalade
and then enjoying the ride to Ty's estate.

"Are you sure that's the right address?"

Bleek rattled off the location to the taxi driver again.

"Okay man, I never took nobody up that way I always
thought that part of the land was blocked off."

"It is to the public."

The cab driver didn't say anything else as he started to drive.
Bleek took his phone out of his pocket and then hovered over
Ty's name. He had run though phones over the past year, but
he always kept his contacts intact. He locked his phone and
then rested his head back as he enjoyed the ride.

When they reached the gate, the man stopped when
he saw men on the land with assault rifles in their hand.

"Uhh buddy can I leave you here? I didn't sign up for
this."

"You see that long ass walk to the house? Hell no. I'll
pay you extra to drive me in just pull up a little so I can put
the code in."

Bleek rolled down his window and then punched the code into the keypad. When the iron gates started to open every man on the lawn turned in the direction of the cab.

"They not about to shoot right?"

The driver nervously asked as he slowly coasted the vehicle towards the house.

"Na, they know I'm either expected or family to know the code. Now once I get out this car, I would haul ass off the property if I were you."

When the cab pulled up to the front of the house, Bleek gave the driver four hundred dollars for a fifty-dollar ride. He got out of the cab and then turned around and started laughing when he saw the man speed down the small hill and out of the gate. He looked up at the house in front of him. A couple of the gun men on the lawn looked at him with shocked eyes but they stood their post.

Bleek took a deep breath before walking up the stairs to the house. He stood in front of the door for a while. He played with the keys in his pocket through the cotton material of the sweatpants that he was wearing. He felt like it would be disrespectful to use his key. Especially since he hadn't spoken to Ty since the night he entered into his home with the note that Toya had sent to Leah's grave site.

He knew that if anyone experienced the mourning of him the worst that it was Ty. Not only did he feel the pain of losing a brother, but he also felt the guilt of thinking continuously of the last time that they were in the same room. He started to take his keys out of his pocket but then he decided not to. He rang the doorbell and then clasped his hands together in front of him.

"Uncle Leek?"

Bleek looked down and saw Paige standing at the open door. She had just turned six years old a few months prior.

"Hey baby girl."

"Paige what the hell did I tell you about answering the door. I don't care if Doc McStuffins is outside do not open my damn door for anyb—"

Toya pulled the door open wider to see who was outside and her words caught in her throat when she saw who was on her doorstep.

"Paige go in the kitchen with Magdala, your sister and brother."

"But mommy I missed uncle Leek—"

"Paige, go!"

Paige jumped at the base in her mother's voice and then rushed off into the back of the house.

"How is this possible?" she whispered once Paige was out of sight.

"I had to do it sis. It had to be done."

Toya stepped outside and then closed the door behind her. She was blocking off her home to him. He tilted his head to the side when he saw her do it.

"The shit almost broke him. I had to beg Magdala to come back to help with the kids because for months he spent his days fucking drinking and lounging around in sorrow. You popping up here is going to do what? What the fuck did you think coming here was going to do? Mend shit, huh?"

She crossed her arms over her body because she needed to know. She needed to know what made him think that coming to her home after faking his death and then being gone for a year would do. Bleek screwed his face in anger because in his mind, she was the cause of it all. Had she not sent that letter of sins to Leah's gravesite there would not have been a Chiva Blanca.

"You not about to jump down my fucking throat when this shit is your fault."

"My fault?"

"Yeah, your fault. The fuck you send that letter to a dead ass body for. If you needed to vent you should have gone to a fucking therapist!"

272

"I found the best way to cope with me mourning.
Have you ever mourned anything? You never had to mourn
shit. You don't know what the fuck you put the man you call
brother through."

Bleek bit his bottom lip in anger. He had lost his
grandmother, mother, and his own son. He knew what
mourning was.

"Stop speaking on shit you know nothing of."

"Stop trying to fix some shit that's unfixable. I had to
put him in rehab for the fucking drinking. Every single night
I sat up with him and tried to keep him off the bottle when he
finished the program. The only way you're seeing him is
over my dead body."

Bleek looked at her in disbelief but when he saw that she
braced herself as if she were preparing for him to barge in, he
knew that she was dead serious.

He shook his head up and down. When the anger in
him subsided, he spoke.

"I never disrespected you and I won't start now. You
got it…" he backed away from her, "you fucking got it."
Hearing everything that his best friend had gone through in
his absence had him feeling sick to his stomach. The last
thing that he wanted to do was open old wounds that could
possibly mess with Ty's sobriety.

"Get one of these niggas to drive me back to the airport."

Toya nodded her head and then waved her hand to one of the men that were standing on the lawn. She was thankful that Ty was spending the day with Julian.

"Take one of the trucks and drive him back to the airport."

The man nodded his head as he walked off to a row of trucks that was parked along the side of the house. Toya felt like she could breathe a little, she sighed and when she did tears came to her eyes.

"I had to mourn you too, you know."

For the past year she was blaming herself for what she thought had happened to him as well. She was thankful that Ty was too consumed with blaming himself because had he took a step back and looked at why there was even a Chiva Blanca problem he could have very well blamed her.

In their past he had blamed her for the loss of someone else that was very dear to him, she knew that if he did it a second time that there would be no saving them. Although he didn't want to, Bleek pulled her into his arms. She hugged him tightly. She didn't want to push him away, but she was putting her man first. Or at least that's what she told herself to make it seem alright, she was selfishly putting herself first.

"He just started making progress, I'm sorry bro."

"Na it's cool."

He grabbed the back of her head and then hugged her tighter.

"It's cool."

When he heard the truck pulling up behind him, he knew that it was time to go. He let go of Toya and then started to walk down the stairs. He stood at the back door to the truck for a while before he pulled it open to get in. He knew that Toya was right. A year ago, when he finally decided to take Manny up on his offer he thought of this exact moment. He thought about not being able to reconnect with the people that he loved. He thought about their pain. All of these people he had put before himself but now he was putting himself first.

As the truck drove down the hill and out of the estate, he thought it all. When he was passing the gate leaving, he saw Julian and Ty in a car pulling into the property. The top was down on the old school automobile that Julian was driving. Ty stopped laughing to look into the windows of the truck, but the tints was too dark. Unknowingly Ty was staring his brother in the eyes. Julian pulled the car into the estate and Bleek's driver pulled off. Bleek rested his dome on the headrest. His phone started to ring so he leaned up in the chair to take it out of his pocket.

He saw that it was Eternity Facetime calling him. He smiled inwardly because he was sure that the screen would fill with the face of his daughter as soon as he answered. Quickly he swiped the bar across the screen. As he predicted the drooling face of his four-month-old appeared on the screen.

"Hiiii daddy mamas."

His voice went soft and only for her it would. He thought that the love of his life was Eternity for so long, and she was but as soon as she pushed the little girl with the gummy filled grin on the phone out, she naturally slid in the second spot.

"Hiiii... tell ya momma to get the boogies out ya nose."

276

"She does not have no fucking boogers I just cleaned her nose."

"Tori watch ya damn mouth around my kid," Eternity fussed.

Eternity grabbed the phone and then pushed her healthy shoulder length hair behind her ear.

"You look fine ma. I see Tori and nem still there."

"Yeah check this shit out. Tori talking about moving here."

Bleek smiled, he knew that home wasn't a state or location a true sense of home was the people you were around.

"Oh yeah? I think they should."

"What about all of the businesses that they own in Florida?"

"Ma you know more than anyone that you don't have to be present for your business to run effectively. It's all about who you hire."

She knew that he was right. For the past year they had run all of his mechanical shops and their youth center back home in Brooklyn.

"That's what I said to her big-headed ass."

Bleek heard Tori yell out in the background.

"How does Sha feel about this?"

"I'm good on it shitttt long as I keep getting these fresh ass croissants in the morning I'll live here forever." Bleek started to laugh when he heard Sha's voice in the background

"You gone get fat as fuck like Bleek's ass then what? Then I'ma leave ya ass. Your head is too damn small for you to ever get fat on me."

"Yeah... yeah... yeah you ain't going nowhere cause if you ever try and leave me for one of these fashionista ass Paris men you gone have to explain to the nigga that bullets will fly y'all way whenever y'all out. Is that really what you wanna deal with?"

"I hate ya stupid ass," Tori threw a pillow at Sha. Eternity laughed into the phone.

"Babe... bring ya ass home."

"I'm coming home ma," he smiled as she puckered up her lips and blew him a kiss.

He was on that mushy shit and didn't care. He was finally at a point in his life where he wasn't seeking peace because it had found him. He blew a kiss back her way before he opened the door to exit the truck. Before walking into the airport, he looked back at the beautiful sky. *I'm going home to my family...* he thought just before disappearing into the automatic glass doors.

C. Wilson

THE END

*** Don't forget to leave those reviews ***

Made in the USA
Columbia, SC
09 February 2025

53058642R00167